The MOUNTAIN RESCUE DOG

The Mountain Rescue Dog

JULIETTE FORREST

SCHOLASTIC

Published in the UK by Scholastic, 2022
1 London Bridge, London, SE1 9BA
Scholastic Ireland, 89E Lagan Road, Dublin Industrial Estate,
Glasnevin, Dublin, D11 HP5F

ISBN 978 0702 31364 6

A CIP catalogue record for this book
is available from the British Library.

Printed by CPI Group (UK) Ltd, Croydon, CR0 4YY
Paper made from wood grown in sustainable forests
and other controlled sources.

1 3 5 7 9 10 8 6 4 2

www.scholastic.co.uk

Dedicated to all those
who search and rescue

CHAPTER 1

The shrill ring of the bell brought the children back to life. They leapt up, shouting and laughing, excited that it was the start of the summer holidays. Everyone bumped into each other as they grabbed their bags, eager to flee the room.

Miss Willow bent to pick up a trail of lost things – scraps of paper, a pen top, a hair tie – until she reached Clova's desk. She straightened and pushed her glasses back up her nose.

"You're the only one who hasn't left the classroom as though your life depends on it," said Miss Willow, perching on the edge of a desk. Some of the pineapples on her yellow shirt wrinkled up.

Clova pulled a tight smile. As well-meaning as her teacher was, she was keen to avoid another speech on how much Miss Willow would miss the class. Or worse: one of her heart-to-hearts.

"Have you seen the weather? No sense in rushing out in that, Miss," lied Clova, as she put on a bright red anorak which was several sizes too big for her.

Although they were breaking up for the summer, it had been overcast and rainy for the past three days. The Scottish weather could be unpredictable at the best of times. One minute you could be in the baking sunshine, swatting away midges, and the next you could be sheltering from torrential rain.

"I'm glad I've managed to catch you," said Miss Willow.

Clova stiffened.

"How are things at home?"

"Fine, Miss." Clova avoided the teacher's gaze. It was one of the questions she most dreaded being asked. She had learned quickly that if she spoke the truth, people didn't know what to say, which led to an embarrassingly awkward silence and a look of pity. Either that or she was told everything would be fine, given time. Something Clova couldn't possibly imagine to be true.

"I'm pleased things are better, Clova. You've been through so much. It's only to be expected that you're behind on your schoolwork. Perhaps some extra assignments over the summer would help get you up to speed?"

Rain hammered against the window, distracting Miss Willow, who glanced towards it. Water droplets on the glass changed the houses into glowing circles of light. By the time she turned back, Clova was by the door.

"Dad is relying on me to lend a hand at the hotel. I won't have time for schoolwork. Thanks, though. Bye," she said, ducking out the door.

"Oh … I… Bye then!" said Miss Willow to the empty room.

The last thing Clova wanted was homework over the holidays. She was looking forward to freedom from the lessons she couldn't care less about.

Stepping outside, Clova was stopped in her tracks

by the wind. Her hair whipped around her head and the rain needled her face. Battleship-grey clouds had sailed in. The sky was so low, Clova felt as though she could reach up and touch it. Beyond the dark, slick surface of the playground, she saw adults sitting in cars, fussing over their children as they belted up. The lights from dashboards illuminated their happy faces.

Clova's chest tightened. She averted her eyes.

What she would give for her mum to be parked across the road, waiting for her.

Clova yanked her hood up and shoved her hands deep into her pockets. As she ran down the steps, the rain began to fall in earnest. It awakened the scent of her mum's perfume on the anorak. For a moment, it smelled as though her mum had just hugged her. She raised her eyes to the mountain. It chose to remain hidden from view behind the solid wall of rain.

I wouldn't like to be out on the peaks today, her mum would have said.

Clova walked through the gathering puddles and weaved her way past the last of the stragglers. The Drovers Inn, the hotel where she lived, was about a kilometre out of the village. The bus had already left.

She was relieved to escape the chatter about Megan's end of year party. Clova hadn't been invited. Everyone wanted to let their hair down – hard to do around the sad kid. Grandpa would have a hot mug of tea waiting for her when she got home. Mum always said tea tasted a million times better after you'd been out in the wind and lashing rain.

Clova turned on to the main road and passed the Glenstrome Café, which looked cosy. She caught sight of Sally, sitting at a table with her mum and little brother, who squished his nose up against the glass, turning it into a snout. There would have been a time Clova would have squashed her own nose against it to make them laugh. However, things weren't so great between them nowadays. Sally had become distant because Clova didn't always want to muck around and have a laugh. These days she didn't feel like she was twelve years old any more, and yet, she wasn't a grown-up either. She was trapped in a weird place she couldn't seem to fathom.

Two beams of light flashed at Clova and an old beat-up Land Rover squealed to a halt beside her. The door was flung open because the window would no longer wind down.

"I could spot you a mile off in your mum's coat. We're heading your way," shouted Isla.

Clova ran around the front of the jeep and climbed in. It smelled of leather, soap and farmyard. Isla's job was tending a flock of over a hundred sheep. Her curls were set in rusty tangles and her cheeks had been buffed to a shine by the wind. Isla was one of those people more at home outdoors than indoors.

The rain sounded like marbles hitting the roof.

"Nice day for it," said Isla, clearing the condensation from the windscreen with the back of her hand. The wipers squealed across the glass as if in pain.

Isla's Alsatian, Rannoch, was in the back, his tail thumping against the seat. He pushed his wet nose through the gap and sneezed on Clova. For as long as she could remember she'd always wanted a dog, but her dad had never been keen. She twisted around to pat Rannoch, who was in his bright orange Glenstrome Search and Rescue coat.

"Has there been a call-out?" she asked.

Rannoch closed his eyes in bliss at Clova scratching his favourite spot behind his ear.

"Your grandpa radioed it in. One of the guests hasn't returned from the mountain and your grandpa wants to make sure he's found so he can pay his hotel bill."

Clova stared at her.

"Nearly had you there! Your grandpa's actually really concerned. The missing guest's walking partner arrived back at the Drovers a couple of hours ago and said they'd been separated in the bad weather. Bill and Pete have just left to head up the search and I'm taking Rannoch to the hotel to scent the man's clothing."

Clova had grown up with the Glenstrome Search and Rescue team using the Drovers as a meeting point. Including the Glenstrome Police, there were twelve of them, who volunteered their time to save the lives of others. Amongst them were farmers, a forestry worker, a shop owner and a tour guide – all of them mountaineering enthusiasts. And, of course, there was Rannoch, who scoured Ben Attrin with Isla for the injured and the lost.

Clova's mum had been a Search and Rescue member and her grandpa used to run courses at the hotel, training dogs for the Search and Rescue Dog

Association. Even though her dad had been a brilliant climber, he never joined the team. He was the one who always served up soup, rolls and the occasional dram after a rescue, no matter what time they finally came off the mountain.

Rannoch nuzzled Clova's cheek. They passed the last of the cottages in the village. The trees thrashed about as if they were trying to cast off their leaves.

"Pete and Bill are going to Devil's Gully where the walker was last seen, and the Glenstrome Police team will join them. I'll start by doing a sweep of the moors first. The temperature is dropping; the poor lad is bound to be soaked to the skin."

"Mum said the winds from the north could make the mountains as cold as the Arctic."

"You'd better believe it. Even though it's summer, the weather is unpredictable, often changing in the blink of an eye, which catches hikers and climbers out: experienced or otherwise."

"I think the walker is very lucky because he has Rannoch."

Isla cracked a smile. "You'll be hard pushed to find a nose as fine as his. We've already attended loads of call-outs this year and it's only June. Mind you, at the grand old age of eight, he's due for a well-earned retirement soon."

"I can't imagine the team without him," said Clova. Her stomach knotted at the thought.

"Me neither."

Rannoch's ears pricked up. He whined and clamped his jaw shut as if agreeing.

"The team will train up another dog when the time comes."

Isla checked her rear mirror. A coach full of tourists was directly behind them. The rain had closed in. Clova felt sorry the visitors wouldn't know they were right beside such an imposing mountain or that waterfalls tumbled over its cliffs like white icing sugar.

Clova shifted in her seat as the jeep swept around the hairpin bend, the lights of the Drovers fizzing in the distance.

"How's your dad?" asked Isla.

Clova knew Isla meant well, but she wasn't in the mood to discuss it. A thin line of water wiggled its way down the inside of her window. She wiped it away. "Same."

"It's only been seven months. You know the team

and I are here for you if there's anything you need."

Clova focused on the trees as they whizzed by, hypnotized by them.

They turned off the road, and crossed a small bridge. Isla swung the jeep sharp right into the hotel's car park, the headlights illuminating the shaking leaves of the rowan trees. The gravel crunched under the Land Rover's wheels. The Drovers' walls were moon-white and all the windows downstairs flickered an electric orange colour. The weather was so awful, Grandpa had lit the fires for the guests.

Rannoch stretched, sensing what was expected of him.

As Clova got out of the Land Rover, she heard the river at the front of the hotel, pounding over the rocks. Isla grabbed her kit from the boot, putting on her waterproofs and a head torch. The door to the hotel opened and yellow light spilled out from it. Clova's grandpa hurried over, clutching a plastic bag.

"No sightings of the walker yet, and the forecast is heavy rain," he said.

Grandpa took a jumper out of the bag and presented it to Rannoch, who buried his nose in the wool. Grandpa had told her that dogs' noses had around two-hundred-and-twenty-five million scent receptors and humans only had five million. This meant Rannoch could detect things in the air as tiny as human skin cells. Clova couldn't begin to imagine how amazing the world must smell to a dog.

"I'll radio if there's news from Devil's Gully," said Grandpa.

Isla checked for the walkie-talkie, and lengthened Rannoch's leash. "I'll be ready for a bowl of your lentil soup when I get back," she said, cheerily.

"We'll keep the fire in the bar going for you," replied Grandpa.

Isla stepped back to focus her attention on Rannoch, who waited patiently, ears pricked up for his next command. She tapped the dog's side to let Rannoch know their work was about to commence. She gave him one final sniff of the missing man's jumper. "Go, seek!" she said in a loud voice. Rannoch barked in excitement, champing at the bit to get started. Together, they set off at a brisk pace, Rannoch out in front. Isla waved at Clova and her grandpa before she disappeared from view.

"Come on, you can have some tea by the fire. What better way is there to start your summer holidays?" said Grandpa as they made their way towards the Drovers.

The wind sounded mournful as it blew over the mountain and rushed across the moors.

"Do you think the walker will be OK?" asked Clova, shivering at the thought of him out there, alone.

Grandpa put his arm around her and drew her in towards him. "I think returning the lost and injured to their loved ones is in our blood."

At that very moment, Clova knew for certain she wanted to save lives on the mountain. Just like her mum had.

CHAPTER 2

Grandpa burst into the room and switched the light on. "We have an emergency, Clova."

She woke with a start and blinked at her grandpa. She'd stayed up late, waiting to see if there was news from the team. Even though it was the holidays, her dad had packed her off to bed at midnight, much to her annoyance. She had sat by her bedroom window, scanning the moors for the flash of a torch. Finally, when her eyelids had become too heavy to keep open, she had admitted defeat and crawled into bed.

"Is it the walker? Did Rannoch find him?" she asked.

"He's safe, but his pride is bruised."

Clova didn't move a muscle as she waited to hear the rest of the story.

"The lad's boots had seen better days. The soles were worn and he slipped on wet rock at the base of the mountain and hurt his ankle. Fortunately, he had his wits about him and found shelter. He put a spare hat on his hiking stick, so he could wave it about to attract attention. Rannoch had locked on to his scent and found him. When Isla saw a hat moving through the air and heard wailing, she thought the man was a banshee."

Grandpa's eyes sparkled. They were exactly the same shade of blue as her mum's had been. Sometimes this caught Clova by surprise because it was like her mum was looking back at her.

"Is Isla OK?" Clova asked.

"Your dad served her three bowls of lentil soup in the early hours of this morning. When she finally left, he had to bolt the door behind her to stop her from sneaking back for more."

Clova rolled her eyes at her grandpa. "If the walker's OK, and Isla and Rannoch are fine, then what's the emergency?"

"Breakfast starts in forty minutes and we're out of sausages and eggs. It slipped your dad's mind to order them."

"Again?" said Clova. Her dad had been forgetting to do lots of things these days.

"I need you to go to Stoneburn Farm. I've telephoned ahead so Mrs Cairncross is expecting you. She's kindly agreed to donate some food for our guests. I'd go myself, only I need to set up the dining room."

Clova's parents had run the Drovers all her life. These days Dad retreated to his room during the day, preferring to work the night shift at the hotel. Clova suspected he did this because there would be fewer guests to have to talk to. Grandpa had moved in at the start of the year and was practically running the place single-handed. There was dust gathering on mantelpieces, cobwebs dangling from ceilings; some of the clocks had stopped and pictures hung squint on the walls. The place smelled more of smoke from the fires than of her mum's homemade lavender room spray. But the guests were sure of a warm welcome, and Grandpa's knowledge of the area – from its wildlife to all the best walking and climbing routes – beat anything you'd ever find in a guidebook. He knew every nook and cranny of the moors and mountains.

"There will be a sausage and egg roll in it for you as a reward," Grandpa added.

"In that case, I'll be back before you know it." Clova leapt out of bed and threw her sweatshirt on, inside out.

*

Clova ran through the field behind the Drovers, startling some crows. She spied the white flashes of rabbits' tails as they disappeared down into their burrows. To the side of her, the moors with their small shimmering lochans stretched all the way to the birch woodland. Ben Attrin rose up behind the trees, its stony plateau touching the blue sky.

Clova spotted something sparkling on the ground. She crouched to study a spiderweb that hung between two stalks of grass like a hammock, glistening with dew drops. She remembered her mum telling her that the silk contained vitamin K which helped to stop bleeding and speed up healing. The Romans had even used them as bandages to wrap around their war wounds. Her mum had found it curious that something which was a death trap for insects could also be used to heal.

Her mum had truly cherished everything outside of the Drovers, from the tiniest insects to Scotland's largest mammal – the red deer. She had taken Clova on nature rambles across the moors and up the mountain, showing her foxes, badgers, roe deer, pine martens, blue hares, red squirrels, ptarmigans, snow buntings, golden plovers, curlews and snipes. The buzzards' cries could be heard all around. With their impressive wingspan, they always excited guests at the hotel, who mistook them for golden eagles. Her mum used to give her dad an earful for letting them go home thinking they'd been lucky enough to see one.

The moors might appear like a solid slab of brown, but when the sun came out the landscape transformed into a riot of caramels, rusts, golds, browns, greens and purples. The peat bogs acted like giant sponges, absorbing the abundance of rainwater. Clova's mum had pointed out where to find yellow, green, orange, red and crimson mosses. As well as sage-green bog myrtle, delicate white tufts of cottongrass that resembled miniature clouds floating on stalks, the showy pinks of sundew and canary-yellow bladderwort – which her dad always used to say sounded like the name of a villain from James Bond.

He never jokes about anything these days, she thought.

Clova climbed the dry-stone wall and paused to glance at the highest peak, which even in summer, wore a wreath of snow. The mountain looked friendly today – as if it would keep all those who ventured on to it safe. Sometimes, when she stared hard enough at Ben Attrin, she thought she could see the outline of her mum's face on the side of the plateau. She half closed her eyes and reached out a finger to trace the shape.

Clova didn't want to be late back at the Drovers, otherwise Grandpa would be behind on the breakfast orders. She leapt down from the wall and tore through another field. Yesterday's rain still clung to the long grass which darkened the hem of her jeans. The sheep paused their munching to eye her warily. Finally deciding she wasn't to be trusted, they trotted off further up the slope, their tails flapping behind them.

Crossing the burn, Clova puffed her way up the embankment to the single-track road that wound its way through the moors to Loch Glenstrome. She spotted a wrought iron sign with *Stoneburn Farm* on it and hurried up the pitted drive, dodging large clumps of mud that had fallen from a tractor's wheels. The farmhouse was built from wolf-grey stone that had proved sturdy enough to weather every storm the mountain had thrown at it.

Entering the courtyard, a movement caught Clova's eye. In front of an old wooden barn, a black-and-white collie paced up and down. As soon as the collie caught sight of her, the strangest thing happened. Instead of rushing to greet Clova – or barking and wagging its tail – the dog's ears flattened and its tail tucked between its legs. The collie sloped off into the barn, dragging a chain behind it. Clova had never seen such a sorry-looking creature. She hurried over to the building and stuck her head inside. The chain was attached to a pillar and there was a bed of fresh straw on the ground beside it. She stepped forward. The dog had snuck into the shadows behind a stack of wooden crates. Clova got down on her hands and knees to see if she could coax the collie out from its hiding place.

"Hullo!" she said, as if the collie was an old friend. "What are you doing in here?"

The dog's ears raised, but it didn't back off. Its nose was black and shiny, and wiggled about all over the place. Its eyes were large and the same colour as the resin from pine trees. The collie studied her, curiously. One of its ears flopped down over its eye. Its fur was sticking up all over the place in unruly black tufts. She smiled, utterly enchanted with the funny little furball. "I'm Clova. I wonder what your name is?"

Clova could tell the collie was in two minds about her, so she remained perfectly still. It seemed to work as the dog crept towards her. Just as the collie plucked up the courage to sniff her outstretched hand, Clova heard footsteps approaching.

The dog shuffled away into the dark.

"What on earth are you doing?" said a voice.

Clova came out from behind the crates, jumped to her feet and brushed the straw from her jeans. "Nothing!"

"I see you've met the stray," said Mrs Cairncross.

"Stray?"

“We found it roaming the fields. I took it to the vet to have its microchip scanned and was given Malachy Bain’s address. He farms the land next to us. Unfortunately, we don’t see eye to eye after a boundary issue we’ve been having. When I knocked on his door, he wasn’t exactly pleased to see me. Then he remarked the collie was a *runner* who attempted to escape so much he said it should have been called ‘Houdini’. Swore the dog was useless and slammed the door in my face.”

Clova’s eyes widened.

“Unfortunately, the local dog rehoming centre is full, so we’re holding on to it until a space becomes available. They’ve said it could be a while because the demand for pets is low during the summer holidays.”

“Why is that?”

“People would rather be away – not stuck at home settling in a new dog.”

“That’s so sad,” said Clova.

How awful not to be wanted, she thought.

“The rehoming centre is going to have their work cut out for them. It’s clearly not used to people and it has never been house trained.”

“Is the dog a he or a she?”

"It's a boy."

"Does *he* need to be chained up?"

"Only a couple of weeks ago, Malachy Bain shot a dog that had attacked his sheep."

Clova gasped in horror. "Won't he go to jail for that?"

Mrs Cairncross shook her head. "In the eyes of the law he was acting to protect his sheep – some of which had been killed by the dog. Dogs are capable of inflicting terrible damage on livestock. Keeping him chained up is far from ideal, but it's … I mean *he's* much safer here for the moment until someone can take him."

"How old is he?"

"The vet thought anything up to twelve months or so."

Mrs Cairncross blinked a few times as though an idea had come to her at that very moment. "You wouldn't have room for him at the Drovers, would you?"

"I'd love a dog," answered Clova without hesitation. "Dad's not keen, though. He said he'd be the one left looking after it because I'd move away to college, or leave to find a job." She sighed. "I don't think he's a dog person. The only one he seems to tolerate is Rannoch."

"The whole of Glenstrome loves Rannoch. If he keeps on saving lives at the rate he does, there will be a statue erected in his honour on the village square."

"Isla would love that." Clova pictured a bronze cast of Rannoch, posing regally with his nose in the air as he gazed up at the mountain.

"We'd never hear the end of it."

Clova peered back into the shadows of the barn, curious. She wished she could see the dog again.

"Your grandpa tells me you are on a mission to stop hungry guests from rioting at the Drovers. I'd better not keep you."

Clova gave one last glance in the direction of the crates, then reluctantly followed Mrs Cairncross to the back door of the kitchen where she was handed a bag laden with food.

"There are pork sausages, two dozen eggs – freshly laid by the girls this morning, and some bacon. That should be enough to fuel your guests up the mountain and back."

"Grandpa will see you right next time you're in the Drovers."

"You tell him I don't require payment. He can give me a bowl of his lentil soup when I'm next in."

"Bye, Mrs Cairncross," Clova said as she flicked her eyes over to the barn. Before she could stop herself, the words blurted out from her mouth. "Mrs Cairncross? Perhaps as a thank you for the food, I could walk the collie?"

Mrs Cairncross hesitated. "I wouldn't want to risk him bolting. He's not comfortable with me yet."

"It was just a thought," said Clova. Her heart sank. She would have loved to see the dog again. "Bye then, Mrs Cairncross." She stuck her hands in her pockets and began to head off down the drive.

The farmer's wife noticed the disappointment that had flashed across Clova's face. Heaven knows she could do with some cheering up after losing her mum in such a tragic way. Perhaps it would do her a bit of good spending some time with the dog.

"On second thoughts..." shouted Mrs Cairncross after the girl.

Clova halted and swung around.

"Why don't you come and visit. The dog needs to get used to being around people."

"Seriously?" said Clova. Her face lit up as she grinned from ear to ear. All traces of disappointment disappeared. "See you tomorrow, Mrs Cairncross!"

She took off at speed, feeling lighter than a feather. She bounded through the fields, alarming the sheep, and threw herself back over the stone wall, sending the crows skywards. Clova was so excited she'd get to see the collie again. Although he'd been shy, the dog had shown some interest in her. She was quite sure they would become firm friends in no time. Clova couldn't help it. She pictured him chasing her through the fields – the best of friends – without a care in the world. Clova laughed at the thought and twirled around on the spot, nearly dropping the bag. She couldn't remember the last time she'd felt so happy and carefree. And all because of the collie!

Clova stopped her daydreaming. Grandpa would be upset with her if the breakfasts were late. She raced across the grass, dandelions losing their fluffy heads in her wake. Clutching the food, she darted along the side of the hotel, burst in through the door, kicked off her shoes, rounded the corner and ran slap bang into her dad. The bag flew out of her hand and hit the floor.

There was a distinct crack of eggs breaking.

"Clova! What have I told you about running in the hotel?" Her dad scowled at her. He bent to pick up the bag and peered inside it. "Make sure you clean up the mess. What a waste of good eggs." He didn't ask her how she was. Or what she had planned for the day. Or thank her for fetching the guests' breakfasts. A look would always creep into his eyes. He was uncomfortable in her presence. She had become a nuisance to him that was to be avoided.

The lightness that had been inside her vanished. Clova heard the heavy tread of her dad's footsteps disappearing up the stairs. The hallway seemed to brighten after he'd left. It was like he had his own weather system around him which was either gloomy or stormy.

She made her way to the kitchen and removed the bacon and sausages from the bag, wiping the egg off with a cloth. Only a couple of the eggs had smashed, which she binned. She cleaned the rest of them up and placed them into the slots on the fridge door. Clova took the bag over to the sink to rinse. She turned the tap on and, without thinking, raised her head to look out the window. A flash of anger stabbed her heart. For a fleeting moment, Clova wished she couldn't see Ben Attrin. She would have given anything for it to be hidden behind another wall of cloud and rain. Because that way, she wouldn't have to look at the mountain that had claimed her mum's life.

CHAPTER 3

Clova woke to the sound of familiar voices. She dressed in a hurry and raced down the stairs to find Isla and Pete at the reception desk. Clova wondered if someone else had run into trouble on the mountain.

"No need to look so worried," said Pete. "We're doing training exercises today with volunteers."

The Glenstrome Search and Rescue team never stopped: if they weren't out saving lives, they were practising how to become better at it. Clova had volunteered for them with her mum. One time, she'd had to hide behind a boulder in the woods and wait for Rannoch to find her, and another time, she'd had her leg bandaged in a first aid exercise, and was carried by stretcher over the moors, which was not as comfortable as it might sound. She'd taken part in some river exercises too, where she'd been rescued. The water had been so cold she'd had to wear a wetsuit.

"Good morning," said Isla. "Your jumper's on back to front, *sleepyhead*."

Clova grinned at her, sheepishly.

"Your grandpa is making us his bacon butties, which happen to be the finest in all the land," said Isla.

"Flattery about my rolls will get you extra tomato ketchup every time," said Grandpa, bumping through the kitchen doors and handing two paper bags over to Isla and Pete. "Sorry for the wait. Breakfast has been hectic this morning. Being the start of the holidays, we're fully booked. There are napkins in the bags and I've put an extra sausage in for Rannoch."

"Where's my sausage? Don't I get one too?" said Pete, pretending to look hurt.

"The day you find a missing person on the mountain with your nose is the day you've earned yourself free sausages from me," said Grandpa, laughing, as he headed off to the dining room.

There was a whining noise outside. Clova went to open the door. Rannoch bounded in, wagging his tail. She crouched and scratched his neck, which made his back paw thump against the floor. Rannoch being so at ease made her think of the collie and how differently he had acted – as though he had been afraid of her. She was longing to see him again. Clova hoped he'd be less shy this time, and that she'd be able to take him out for a walk. He must be fed up of being stuck in a barn. Clova became lost in her thoughts, once again picturing herself and the dog striding across the moors together. His ears were raised, listening to her every command, as he gazed at her the same way Rannoch looks at Isla.

Isla's laugh snapped Clova out of her thoughts. Rannoch had trotted straight over to her side and nudged the pocket with the breakfast roll in it.

"I see your nose is working overtime already, Rannoch. Let's put it to good use and find all the volunteers today, shall we?" said Isla.

Rannoch raised his ears and barked, running to the door as Isla and Pete said their goodbyes.

Clova entered the kitchen and helped herself to some scrambled egg and toast. After wolfing it down, she set about doing the chores she'd been given at the Drovers over the summer. She didn't mind earning some pocket money – and anything beat being stuck in school. She cleared the last of the breakfast dishes away from the dining room and stacked them in the dishwasher, belting out some songs as she imagined running with the collie alongside the river. Grandpa ducked into the kitchen, hunting for a spare lightbulb for one of the guest's rooms, and then disappeared off again.

Clova swept out the ashes from the fireplaces, which made her sneeze violently. This gave Mrs Burnett from Room 10 such a terrible fright, she dropped her book. Clova reset the fires with pieces of scrunched-up newspaper and kindling, just the way Mum had shown her. She tidied up all the pamphlets of local tourist attractions at reception, and made sure the toilets had soap and clean hand-towels. Clova collected the bedding from the rooms of checked-out guests and carried them over to the last outbuilding where the laundry was. She emptied the washing machine of clean sheets, and refilled it with the next load. As she hung out the washing, she spotted a roe deer grazing in the field. It raised its reddish-brown head and flicked its ears as it chewed on grass. Mum used to say seeing one was a reminder you should be kind to others. This always made Dad give her a look as if she'd lost her marbles, so she'd cuff him on the arm, and the pair of them would burst into laughter. Clova glanced up at Dad's room. The curtains had been closed ever since Mum died. She was certain it was so Dad didn't have to look at the mountain.

Clova went back inside. Grandpa was busy checking in two new guests. By the outdoor clothing they were wearing, she guessed they were climbers. She saw her opportunity and snuck into the kitchen, where she hurried over to the fridge. Rannoch would do anything for some chicken and she hoped the collie would be exactly the same. She pinched a few pieces, put them in a bag and shoved it into her pocket. Clova poured herself a giant glass of chocolate milk, downing it in one. Grandpa entered the kitchen and leant on the table, watching her as she tidied her glass away into the dishwasher.

"What are you up to?" asked Grandpa.

"Nothing," she said. Truth was, she liked having the dog as a secret all to herself. Since her mum had died, it felt as though she was living in a fishbowl and everyone was watching her every move to see how she was. At times it was suffocating and she longed to escape from prying eyes.

Grandpa drummed his fingers on the tabletop. "There's something different about you today."

Clova pushed down her fizzing excitement about seeing the collie and shrugged. "I'm just the same as I was yesterday, and the day before that."

Grandpa narrowed his eyes. "No. I heard you singing, earlier. Although *caterwauling* would be a more accurate description."

"Grandpa!" said Clova, exasperated.

He laughed.

"Would it be OK if I went out?" she asked.

"What about lunch?"

"I had a big breakfast."

"You're not meeting a *boy*, are you?" Grandpa threw his hands up in mock horror.

"No!" said Clova. Her cheeks flushed.

“Just as well then,” he replied. “Because you’re sporting a giant chocolate moustache on your top lip.”

Clova used the sleeve of her jumper to wipe her mouth.

“Your dad and I are grateful for your help. You deserve a bit of time off after all the work you’ve done today.” Grandpa switched the kettle on. “Go on. Run wild and free – but be back no later than four p.m. Or else. And take your phone. And don’t be talking to any strangers. Or pinching any more chocolate milk.”

Clova found her phone, put on her coat and stepped outside. The wind swirled around, bringing the trees, bushes, flowers and grass to life. Her stomach filled with butterflies at the thought of seeing the collie again. Clova hared through the fields, faster than the clouds chasing each other across the sky. She only halted once, to see if she could spot any of the Search and Rescue team on the moors, but they were hidden by the lengthening shadows on the mountain.

At Stoneburn Farm, she jogged up the driveway, and rounded the corner into the courtyard, startling the stray. He crouched down low to the ground and crawled into the outbuilding, his chain dragging behind him. Clova cursed herself for giving the poor dog a fright. She crept in after him, careful not to make any sudden movements. The collie's chain led behind the crates where he was hiding again. Clova peered into the gap and glimpsed his thick black fur sticking out all over the place. He didn't look as sleek as Rannoch or neatly coiffured like some of the dogs in the village. The collie looked a bit tatty as if he'd been left out in the wind and the rain. Clova's eyes lit up.

"Tatty," she said, liking the sound of it very much. "I'm going to call you 'Tatty'."

Tatty's tail wagged, which she took as a sign he liked it too. She kneeled in the straw and reached her hand out to stroke him. He backed off, and shook himself.

Funny. Dogs usually like me, she thought.

Clova sighed and plonked herself on the ground. The barn creaked and shifted. A draught tickled the back of Clova's neck. She decided to sit it out. Tatty would become so bored, he was bound to show himself.

After an hour had been and gone, the dog hadn't moved a muscle. Sparrows chattered in the eaves of the barn, full of gossip. A tiny brown mouse flashed across the floor and disappeared behind some rusted machinery.

If a mouse hadn't been afraid to show itself, then why couldn't Tatty? she thought.

Clova waggled her foot from side to side to stop the pins and needles. Shoving her hands into her pockets, she felt something at her fingertips. She took a piece of chicken out of the bag, stretched her arm behind the wooden crates and waved the tasty morsel around.

"Tatty!" she said. "Here, boy!"

The dog stirred.

Clova placed some bits of chicken in a line that led to the dog's bed and walked over to the doorway, where she stood in silence for ages. Finally, Tatty's chain scraped against the side of the crates as he stole forward. Clova hardly dared breathe. At last, her patience was finally rewarded by a black, shiny nose sniffing at the chicken. Clova willed Tatty to show himself. As his muzzle came into view, Clova's phone rang, which sounded deafening. Tatty darted back into his hiding place, leaving the chicken untouched. Clova muttered under her breath as she dived outside to answer the call.

"Hullo?"

"Where are you?" asked her dad.

"Grandpa said it was OK to get some fresh air. I've done my chores." Her dad tolerated Rannoch, but if she mentioned Tatty, he'd only find an excuse to give her grief: something he was good at these days.

"Your grandpa told you to be back by four p.m."

Clova checked her watch, horrified to discover it was four twenty p.m.

"Are you on the moors? I asked you not to go there; you know they're dangerous," he said.

"I'm nowhere near the moors," she said, unable to hide her irritation. "I lost track of time, that's all."

A silence fell between them.

"There's a weather front closing in. More rain is on the way and visibility will be poor. Come home, Clova. Now!" Her dad's voice crackled in her ear.

She was certain when her mum had been alive, he had never been as bad as this. Checking up on her all the time. Convinced she wasn't able to look after herself.

"I'm on my way," she said, hanging up. As she peaked into the barn one last time, she saw all the pieces of chicken had disappeared.

Tatty must have snuck out when she wasn't looking!

She grinned. She hadn't quite managed a walk with him – but this was a start. "Bye, Tatty. I'll be back soon," she said before she left. As she passed the chicken coop, she waved at Mrs Cairncross, who was singing to the hens as she dished out their feed.

CHAPTER 4

Grandpa was at the stove in the kitchen, blowing on a spoonful of sauce to cool it down before he tasted it.

"The wanderer returns," he said, his mouth full.

"Are you going to give me a hard time as well?" she said.

"I wasn't planning on it," he answered. "You have impeccable timing for a late person. Dinner is served."

Clova kicked off her shoes and dumped her red coat over the chair at the end of the table. If Mum had been here she would have told Clova to hang up her jacket, tidy her shoes away and wash her hands.

Grandpa opened a drawer and handed Clova some cutlery to set the table with. "Your dad was just checking to see you were OK because you weren't here when you said you'd be."

"The sheep out there have more freedom than I do," she grumbled.

Grandpa dished out the spaghetti and tomato sauce. Lately his son-in-law and granddaughter had been at each other's throats. And he'd begun to feel like the United Nations trying to keep the peace between them. "Would you like me to have a word?" he asked.

Clova shook her head. Her dad was like the game, Buckaroo. The more problems he was weighed down with, the more likely he was to lose it. If he *bucked,* he might ground her or worse – sell up the hotel, which he'd already threatened to do a couple of times. Her insides clenched at the thought. That would be a real disaster as the land outside connected Clova to so many treasured memories of her mum. It also dawned on her that if they moved away she wouldn't get to see Tatty again. He was the first thing to make her happy in a long time. In fact, when she was with him, she forgot about all her other woes. She could be herself again.

"You know you can always chat to me about your mum." Grandpa slid her dinner over the table to her. She gave him a quick smile. Every time she had wanted to talk about her mum, she'd struggled to find the right words. Then a million different emotions would bubble up and all she could do was cry. It was messy and embarrassing and best not to go there if she could help it. Steam wafted up off the plate, warming Clova's face. She breathed in the scents of tomato, pepper, grated cheese and basil. She studied her grandpa as he tucked into his meal. There was something else she wanted to talk to him about. He'd run the Search and Rescue dog training course at the Drovers for as long as she could remember. There wasn't anything he didn't know about dogs.

"How do you get a dog to like you?" she asked, casually, twirling spaghetti around her fork.

"Make them laugh." His expression remained unchanged, but his blue eyes twinkled mischievously.

"*Grandpa!*" she said. "I'm being serious."

"You're not going to try and persuade your dad into getting one, are you?"

"I'm just curious, that's all," she said, keeping tight-lipped about Tatty.

He could tell by the way his granddaughter stared at him that she was keen to hear his answer. Clova looked at him exactly the same way her mum used to when she was this age. He cleared his throat. "If you want a dog to like you, then they have to trust you. You have to take care of their needs such as exercise, feeding and grooming. And train them so they understand the basic commands. Dogs work extremely hard to understand what we're asking of them and very often we give them conflicting messages."

"Like how?"

Grandpa put down his fork. "Take something like recall. We reward a dog for coming back to us when we call their name. But if the dog becomes distracted, and runs off to play with another dog, the owner gives their dog a row when they finally do return. That's because the owner sees it as a fail. But all this does is confuse the dog. Why should they come back at all if they're going to get into trouble for it?"

"You should always praise a dog for returning to you?"

"That's right."

She made a mental note to make a fuss over Tatty when he came to her. *If I can ever coax him out from behind the crates,* she thought.

Grandpa carried on, "When training is a positive experience for the dog, you'll find they're keen to repeat what's been asked of them."

Clova remembered how Tatty had slunk off into the barn with his tail between his legs. "What about a dog who's not had the best start in life? Will they ever be OK with people again?"

"It'll take longer to earn their trust. I've not met a dog yet who can't be rehabilitated with encouragement, kindness and the proper training."

Clova polished off her meal and sat back. For the first time in ages, she didn't feel the pain of her grief gnawing at her stomach. She couldn't help herself. She imagined her and Tatty running over the moors together – Tatty's tail straight up in the air.

"Earth to Clova?" Grandpa brought her back to the kitchen. "A scoop of chocolate ice cream for desert?"

She nodded.

"Good!" he replied. "It'll give you the energy to help me with the dishes."

"I might need an extra scoop for that, Grandpa."

The doors swung open and Clova's dad appeared, shoulders stooped, hands in his pockets. "The bar is quiet this evening. People must be staying away because of the weather."

Outside, the moors had changed colour as if the sun had been stolen from the sky. The mountain was once again wrapped in a shawl of grey mist.

"Have all the guests returned OK?" asked Grandpa.

"All except for the gents from rooms 1 and 8, but they're dining out at the Glenstrome Café tonight."

"There's some dinner in the oven for you," said Grandpa. He handed Clova a bowl of ice cream with two scoops in it. "I'll take over in the bar. There's no hurry, so don't go giving yourself indigestion, Jim," he said, winking at Clova.

Clova pulled a face at Grandpa. She watched the doors close behind him. Trapped in the kitchen, she sat poking the ice cream with her spoon until it softened. The fact Dad was quiet meant he was building up to say something.

He brought his plate out of the oven and sat opposite her. He ground some black pepper over the top of the pasta. "Do you want to tell me where you sloped off to this afternoon?"

"Not really." She put her spoon down.

"So you *were* on the moors." He stared at her.

"I wasn't anywhere near them – but even if I had been, I know them like the back of my hand."

"Clova, you're twelve years old. Experienced hikers run into trouble out there all the time. The moors are every bit as dangerous as the mountain."

"I wasn't on the moors. How many times do I have to tell you?" she said, raising her voice in frustration.

Her dad slammed his hand down on the table. "Look, I need to know where you are at all times."

"Why?"

"So I can help if you're in trouble."

"I can keep myself perfectly safe. Mum showed me how," she said, her eyes flashing with anger.

"That's just it, Clova. Your mum had been saving lives for years. I doubt there was anyone more experienced than her in the Search and Rescue team. But when up against the elements, even she couldn't protect herself. I believe she thought she could, but no one can," shouted her dad. "And now I'm the only parent you've got left, so what I say goes. You're not going out again unless you tell me where you are off to first. And if you're ever late home again, I can't trust you. And if I can't trust you, how on earth can we keep on living in a place like this where there is danger lurking around every corner?" Her dad pushed his plate away from him.

Clova's chair flew back as she jumped to her feet. "I'm sorry to be such an inconvenience to you now Mum's no longer here."

Her dad's mouth dropped open, but no words came out.

Clova fled from the table. She burst through the kitchen doors and shot up the stairs. Two of the guests flattened themselves against the walls to let her past as she marched along the hallway. She stormed into the family quarters and entered her room, slamming the door so hard something splintered. Flinging herself on to the bed, she buried her face into her pillow. She hated that she'd have to get her dad's approval on every move she made this summer. If her dad ever found out about Tatty, there was no way she'd be allowed to see him again.

Dad won't be happy until I am locked up like a prisoner in my room, she thought, bitterly.

She wished with every fibre of her being that her mum was still alive and everything could go back to the way it had been before the accident.

CHAPTER 5

Clova checked her dad's door was closed and slunk past it. The less she saw of him today, the better. When she thought about the argument they'd had, anger bubbled up from the pit of her stomach. He treated her like a five-year-old. He couldn't discuss things. He could only make threats about leaving everything she knew and loved at the Drovers.

She padded down the stairs and spotted Isla in the car park. Outside, Rannoch bounded over to Clova and licked her hand before sitting. Staying angry was impossible when he was around. There couldn't have been an emergency call-out because neither Isla nor Rannoch were in their Search and Rescue gear.

"You're up early considering it's the summer holidays," said Isla.

Clova smiled politely. It was even more of a miracle she was awake because she'd hardly slept a wink thanks to the argument with her dad. "I promised Grandpa I'd help with the breakfasts."

"He'll be glad of an extra pair of hands."

"What are you doing?"

"Your dad said it was OK for Search and Rescue to store some replacement equipment in one of the outhouses. You'd be amazed at how much we can lose during a rescue."

Clova wandered over to the Land Rover.

"Want to help?" asked Isla.

Inside the back of the jeep were neatly coiled lengths of climbing rope; a couple of folded up stretchers; some Search and Rescue hi-vis jackets; a spare dog lead; a first aid kit; torches; batteries; blankets; a pile of extra waterproofs; woolly hats and warm clothing. Isla grabbed two of the folded up stretchers and led the way. Clova picked up the rope coils, and stuck her arm through them, carefully, so they didn't unravel. Isla paused up ahead, taking in the mountain and the vastness of the sky surrounding it.

"I'll never tire of that view," Isla said with wonder in her voice as though she was seeing it for the first time.

Clova understood what she meant. Every minute of every day, the mountain's appearance changed. Sometimes it would be bathed in sunlight, looking majestic and inviting, as though you wouldn't even break into a sweat if you wanted to climb to the top. And at other times it would loom over the Drovers, dark and threatening. Warning all those who dared to venture on to it that their lives would be in mortal danger. On those days, when Clova caught sight of the mountain, she wouldn't be able to shake off a sense of foreboding. She knew Ben Attrin possessed different personalities that could change without warning. She knew more than most what it was capable of. But she found it impossible to hate something which her mum had loved so much.

Rannoch settled in the sun, sniffing scents on the breeze as he kept an eye on the comings and goings.

Every time Isla and Clova passed him with armfuls of equipment and clothing, he'd thump his tail against the ground. And when Clova dropped some gloves on the gravel, his ears shot up.

In the outhouse, Isla placed a bundle of clothing in a large sealable container. Clova packed some woolly jumpers and hats into another. Sometimes it wasn't the terrain that killed but the low temperatures. If conditions were freezing, people were in need of warm, dry clothing to help them raise their body temperature so they could ward off frostbite or hypothermia.

As they returned to the Land Rover, Rannoch barked to let them know two guests were in the car park. Clova waved at them.

"Isla? Was training Rannoch easy?" she asked as she grappled with a first aid kit that had become wedged under a pair of muddy boots.

"I wouldn't say that. It took lots of hard work to get him to the level he's at today – and, as you know, we have to maintain his training," answered Isla.

Clova remembered Tatty being skittish at the farm. "How do you get Rannoch to look at you the way he does?"

"Oh, that's easy. I bribe him with sausages," she said, laughing.

Isla had the same sense of humour as Clova's grandpa. She half wondered if Isla and her grandpa had seen so many sad things over the years on the Search and Rescue team that they always made a point of being cheerful.

Isla continued on. "I've been lucky enough to have been around dogs all my life, but the bond with Rannoch is different. It goes deeper."

"Why is that?" Clova was keen to hear what she said because it could help her with Tatty. Rannoch's ears also swivelled forward as if he was interested in Isla's answer.

"I think it's because we work as a team, which means we're in tune with each other. I swear we both know what the other is thinking."

Clova was itching to see Tatty. She felt sure today would be entirely different. That he'd realize she meant him no harm and be pleased to see her. It would be great to get his training off to a good start. To work as a team, together.

"What were the first commands you taught

Rannoch?" asked Clova.

"We practised 'sit', 'down' and 'stay'. Then we moved on to recall, which is slightly trickier."

"Grandpa said you should always praise a dog for coming back to you."

"That's good advice, Clova. I started Rannoch off under the watchful eye of your grandpa. We were in the field behind the Drovers because it was enclosed. I had him on an extra-long lead so he could take his time exploring. It's good for them to have distractions, so they're not just focusing solely on you. If you think about it when you're out and about lots of things constantly vie for their attention."

"Did you just call his name? And wait for him to come to you?"

"I chose one command that I always use, so I don't confuse him. I also had some treats, which I rewarded him with. As much as he loved them, he really responded to me making a big old fuss of him too. I kept my voice soft and was careful not to overwork him because, believe it or not, dogs get sick and tired of doing the same thing over and over again just like us."

"I wish someone had told Miss Willow not to go

over fractions again and again."

Isla laughed. "Poor old Miss Willow!"

Clova rubbed her forehead. "Recall sounds complicated."

"It's all about repeating the training every day in short bursts, and most importantly, keeping it fun for the dog and yourself," said Isla, her voice full of encouragement. She hesitated. Her eyes locked on to Clova's. "Are you getting a dog?"

Clova adored Isla and Rannoch, but didn't want to spill the beans about Tatty just yet. Especially when she'd not even managed to entice the collie out from behind the wooden crates. "I'm just curious about it, that's all."

Isla hefted the last of the boxes up on to the shelf and stepped back to check everything was in order. "You mum once saw you and Rannoch on a walk and said she thought you might end up working with dogs, like your grandpa."

Clova felt a pang of sadness. She wished her mum was here to say that to her in person. She supposed hearing it from Isla was the next best thing.

Isla glanced at her watch. "I have to shoot. Rannoch and I have to bring a couple of sheep off the hills for the vet to examine this afternoon."

Clova walked Isla to the jeep and opened the door for Rannoch to jump inside. Isla started the engine and tooted the horn.

"See you later, alligator," said Clova, waving them off.

"Back in a while, crocodile," Isla shouted.

Curtains twitched as a guest looked out of the window, wondering what all the commotion was about. Clova headed into the Drovers to help her grandpa serve the breakfasts. The guests were lovely and friendly, but she found herself counting down the minutes until she could be with Tatty again.

*

Clova ran up the driveway and slowed as she neared the end of it. This time, she remembered to approach with caution so she wouldn't give the collie a fright. Her heart beat fast. Partly because she'd run the whole way there. But mostly because she'd snuck out without her dad knowing where she was. Grandpa had gone to Fort William to pick up supplies for the hotel and her dad had still been in his room. One of the villagers, Marie, was helping out in the bar and had been chatting to customers when Clova had checked. Isla had told her it was good to keep the training short and fun, so she was certain she could be back at the Drovers before anyone missed her.

When she entered the barn, the dog had vanished. He must have heard her footsteps and slipped behind the crates.

Clova lifted a wooden crate off the pile and placed it on the ground. She moved it away from Tatty to give him some space and sat. When she spoke, she kept her voice soft and steady, "Hullo, Tatty. It's me."

She was a bit dismayed that he was still unsure of her. She remembered what her grandpa had said about that: if you could make dogs laugh, they'd never leave your side. At this point in time, Clova would try anything to get Tatty to trust her. She checked nobody else was around.

"Hey, Tatty? What did one flea say to the other?" she said, pausing to give him enough time to think about the question. "Shall we walk or take the dog?"

Tatty didn't move. Or wag his tail. Or raise his ears.

"What do you get when you cross a sheepdog with a jelly? The collie-wobbles."

Nothing.

Clova sighed and glanced around. Half of the barn was split into pens for animals. The rest of it was filled with straw bales and pieces of farming machinery. Sunlight strobed down through green, mossy windows in the roof. Broken cobwebs encrusted with dust and silvery insect wings puffed in and out as though they were breathing. Her mum would have liked it in there. She preferred barns to posh shopping centres.

Clova decided to break the silence. "You and me have a lot in common, Tatty. All this is different and strange to you because this isn't your home. And my home is all different and strange because Mum's not there any more. I mean, it looks the same. It's full of people, but it feels empty without her there."

Clova leant back against a pillar. This was the first time she'd spoken about how she felt without clamming up. Or breaking down in tears. She decided to continue on. Tatty didn't seem to mind. "Every time I walk into the reception, I keep on thinking I'll see her checking the guests in, or adding a log to the fire, or picking up fallen flower petals, or answering the telephone. If I hear someone humming, I'll think it's her, because she'd put her headphones on and listen to music as she was getting the rooms ready for guests. Once, I thought I heard her laugh. I raced all the way downstairs into the dining room to find it was just one of the guests chatting to Grandpa, who wondered what I was doing gawping at them. If you couldn't find Mum in the hotel, she'd be out the back. Sometimes just gazing up at the mountain. As if she could hear it calling to her or something. Can I tell you a secret, Tatty? Every time I pass a window, I glance out of it, really quick, hoping I'll catch sight of her because this has all been some horrible mistake. Except, she's never there." Clova's voice wavered. "I get it, Tatty. You don't want to come out from behind those crates because everything is unfamiliar and scary when your life has been turned upside down."

Clova stroked the crate absentmindedly, the wood rough under her fingers. "School was awful. The looks of pity. The awkward silences when nobody knew what to say. And there were whispers flying around about my mum. How it had been her fault. That she was selfish putting her life at risk when she had a family. There were kids who spoke about the accident as though they'd seen it with their own eyes. I hate being there. What's the point in working hard? It won't bring her back."

Clova brought her knees up to her chest and hugged them. "If Dad could chain me up, he would. He's worried that I'll go out the door and never return. Just like Mum." The dog stirred and Clova carried on. "So you see, I do understand how you're feeling, a bit. This is no way for you to live. You must be dreaming of the day when you'll be free again."

Clova sat in silence for a while, lost in her thoughts. She heard a scraping noise. Tatty crept out of the shadows. The dog lowered his head and gazed up at her, unsure. His ears were pinned back. A white stripe ran down the middle of his forehead to his nose, which wiggled from side to side as he scented the air. His front paws were white and his back paws black. Tatty's eyes darted around taking in every single detail about her.

Clova's instinct was to reach out and pat him. However, she stopped herself in case he recoiled. She dropped her gaze, so she wasn't staring directly at the collie. Tatty inched closer. He sniffed the ground. He smelled of a mixture of sweet straw, warm buttery popcorn and earth. Tatty was so close to her the hairs went up on her arms.

"You're one lucky fella, Tatty. If you hadn't shown yourself, I was going to sing to you – and that really would have had you running for the hills."

Out of the corner of her eye, Clova noticed Tatty tilting his head as she spoke. He was listening to her every word. Very slowly, Clova sat up straight and reached into her pocket for an old ball of Rannoch's she'd found at the hotel. She'd leave it here for him so he'd have something to play with. She brought it out and held it in her hands for Tatty to see. His head bobbed up and down as he tried to work out what it was. If she rolled it towards him, the dog might panic. She stood and placed the ball on the ground. Tatty backed off a little. She scattered some treats next to the ball as a reward for showing himself. As much as she was desperate to stay, she had to return to the hotel before she was missed.

Clova walked towards the door. By the time she had glanced back, Tatty had eaten the treats. He licked his lips, sniffed at the ball and then raised his head, watching her. An ear flopped down over his eye.

"Bye, Tatty," she said. It was agony leaving him behind.

As Clova crossed the courtyard, Mrs Cairncross appeared. "Nancy, Sorrel, Betsy, Cluck and Mouse have been working overtime."

Clova squinted at Mrs Cairncross.

"You'd be doing me a favour." Mrs Cairncross passed her a weighty bag full of eggs in boxes. "You're making progress, aren't you?"

Clova paused. Mrs Cairncross must be keeping a close eye on her – like everyone else.

"You left the barn whistling," she continued on.

"I've given the collie a name, Mrs Cairncross, and I think he likes it."

"What have you called him?"

"Tatty."

"*Tatty?*" Mrs Cairncross laughed. "That's very fitting."

Clova looked the cheeriest Mrs Cairncross had seen the girl in a while. She could only suppose the dog was doing her some good. "Oh, I meant to say there was a bit of a commotion when I passed the Drovers earlier.

Search and Rescue were in the car park."

Clova froze. Had her dad discovered that she'd snuck out? Were people combing the area for her? She took out her phone. To her relief, there were no missed calls. The team only trained at weekends, so someone must be in trouble. "Thanks for the eggs!" she shouted over her shoulder.

"Try not to scramble them on your way home," Mrs Cairncross watched the girl take off down the path as though she'd just been told the Drovers was on fire.

CHAPTER 6

Clova slipped in the back door and shook off her jacket. She checked the coast was clear before she entered the kitchen. Miraculously, none of the eggs appeared to have broken. She opened the fridge and placed the boxes inside. There were so many, they filled the whole shelf and the slots in the door.

Clova heard a commotion. She left the kitchen and saw some guests standing in reception. She squeezed past two of them to find an elderly lady, who had just been brought in by Search and Rescue members, Pete and Bill. The woman's head had been bandaged, but blood was seeping out and dripped on to her top. Clova had seen her mum and the Search and Rescue team deal with injuries since she was little. The sight of blood or broken bones or frostbite no longer upset her. Her mum had explained that they were just the body's ways of signposting the parts that needed medical attention.

The guests crowded around the woman.

"The dining room is empty," she said.

"Good shout, Clova," said Pete.

Dashing ahead into the room, Clova grabbed a chair for the lady to sit on. Bill and Pete steered the woman over to it. She wobbled before she sat.

The lady had a skirt, cardigan and brogues on. She wasn't dressed for the hills.

"What happened?" Clova asked.

"This is Wilma. She'd veered off the road to avoid a deer, and hit a low wall. Glenstrome Police just happened to be passing and found her car – but there had been no sign of her at the scene of the accident so they called us in," answered Pete.

"Luckily, you hadn't strayed far. Isn't that right, Wilma?"

Wilma managed a smile. Bill squeezed her shoulder, gently, to reassure her.

"Did Isla and Rannoch find her?" asked Clova.

"It's their day off."

"How did you know where Wilma was?"

"All the rain we've been having made our job easier. Bill and I were able to follow Wilma's tracks from her car into the woods. Luckily for us, she'd stopped for a breather."

"Your dad's called the doctor, and she's on her way," said Bill.

Wilma glanced up at them.

"The doctor will make sure you're as good as new, Wilma," said Bill.

"I'm seventy-six. That'll take a miracle," she said. Wilma glanced down and caught sight of the blood on her top. Her hand brushed at it as though trying to wipe it off.

"A head wound can look much worse because the scalp has more blood vessels near the surface of the skin." Pete reached into his first aid kit for an instant ice pack, which he tore open and showed Wilma where to press it against her head. "This will reduce the swelling and stem the bleeding. Bill, any more bandages?"

"We've used all the ones in the kit."

"I know where there are more! And a clean top," piped up Clova. "Shall I go and get them?"

"Please, Clova," said Bill.

Clova hotfooted it into reception, slowing to pass two guests, who were itching to find out what was going on. She slipped out the door just as Dr Cuthbertson pulled up in the car park. Clova waved and ran over to her car.

"Dr Cuthbertson, they're waiting for you in the dining room!"

"Thanks, Clova. How are you?"

"Glad it's the holidays," she answered.

"Clova!"

She whirled around to see her dad hovering in the doorway. "The doctor's not here to chit-chat. She's needed inside," he shouted over.

Dr Cuthbertson touched Clova's arm and gave her a warm smile. "It was lovely to see you," she said, before making her way to the hotel.

Clova knew from her dad's voice that he was rattled.

She glanced back at him as he greeted the doctor, all smiles. Did he know she'd snuck out earlier? Or was he on edge because there'd been an accident?

She hurried around the side of the hotel to the outhouse. She took a box down from the shelf and rifled around inside it until she found a jumper she thought would fit Wilma. Then she opened one of the first aid kits and checked it for bandages. Two rolls should be enough for now. She tidied everything away and sped back to the hotel. It was strange, but doing the same thing her mum used to was comforting.

In the dining room, Dr Cuthbertson was shining a beam of light into Wilma's eyes and asking her lots of questions. Clova handed the bandages over to Pete. "Isla's stored spare equipment in the outhouse next to the laundry. There are also extra clothes and waterproofs if you ever need them."

Pete grinned at her.

Clova's dad came into the room carrying a tray. On it was a large pot of tea, some mugs and a plate of biscuits.

"Your daughter's quick thinking has just seen her promoted to our youngest Glenstrome Search and

Rescue team member," said Pete.

Clova glowed. Being the youngest ever Glenstrome Search and Rescue team member sounded – *amazing*. Beaming with pride, she leant back against a chair, and knocked the doctor's bag over. It fell to the ground with a clatter. Clova stooped to pick up the contents that had scattered over the floor, her cheeks burning.

"Oh, don't worry," said Dr Cuthbertson. "Nothing's broken."

"Clova!" barked her dad. "People can't do their jobs properly with you in the way. And I don't want to hear any more nonsense about her being a *team member.* If others wish to risk their lives on the mountain that's their business. But not my daughter!"

Pete opened his mouth to say something. Bill shook his head at him.

Clova saw red. The dark red of Wilma's blood on her top. The shiny red stone on Dr Cuthbertson's engagement ring. The red flush on her dad's cheeks. As she fled the room, she saw the red tiles around the fireplace, and the red rug that led to the front door. She bolted across the car park. A red car whizzed by as she crossed the road and entered the woods.

Clova slowed down and stopped. Her shoulders heaved as she caught her breath. In amongst the trees, ferns, brambles, bracken and knots of ivy, it was dark and cool. The different hues of green calmed her. She climbed up into the arm-like branches of an oak tree and rested her head against the trunk. Her mum had once told her that trees made noises humans couldn't hear. She listened hard for a while, the bark rough against her ear. She wished her dad would listen to her for once. No matter how much she wanted to, he'd never allow her to join Search and Rescue. And there was no way he'd let her see Tatty either. The collie being stuck in a barn, alone, made her so sad. What had the poor thing done to deserve that?

A bright yellow butterfly flitted past. Clova stared at it, unblinking. She remembered the yellow helicopter landing in the snow at the back of the Drovers. Her dad's hands had gripped her shoulders hard so she couldn't run forward. Mum had been inside the helicopter. Not as a team member, but as the casualty. The lower it had got to the ground, the more snow had been kicked up by it, until Clova could no longer see the helicopter. She could only hear the *whup-whup-whup* of the blades – a sound that had passed straight through her heart.

Clova lost herself in her whirling thoughts. She didn't notice the ground beneath her darken as the sun dipped behind the trees.

"Are you only welcoming the company of squirrels? Or can anyone join you?"

His voice startled Clova. She peered down through the leaves. Her grandpa stood, hands on hips, looking up at her.

"You're back from Fort William?" she said.

"Apparently so."

He didn't wait for an invitation to climb the tree. As he hoisted himself on to the same branch, she shuffled along to make space for him. They sat in silence, admiring the view. The air was still and smelled of damp leaves, wild herbs and aromatic pine needles. There was also a sweet scent floating around like candy floss mixed with liquorish. A thrush sifted through the floor of the forest, searching for dinner. Somewhere, up above, came the lone cry of a buzzard.

"It's a while since I've been in a tree with a lady. The last time was in 1967. Her name was Sheila and I'd persuaded her to go on a date in a conifer tree."

Clova snorted. "Grandpa, why would anyone want to go on a date with you? In a tree?"

"I suspect she'd fallen for my wit, natural charm and devilishly handsome looks."

Clova narrowed her eyes at him.

"The tree I took her to was opposite one that housed an osprey's nest and Sheila was an avid birdwatcher. I spent a fascinating afternoon with the second most beautiful lassie in the Highlands."

"Who was the first?"

"The osprey – she was very fetching as I recall." He laughed. "I'm pulling your leg. The first most beautiful lassie was your grandmother, of course."

Her gran had died when she was young, but she felt like she'd known her because of Mum and Grandpa's stories about her. He always spoke about her gran with so much affection in his voice. Sometimes Clova would notice a faraway look in his eyes, as though he was lost in a memory of her and not in any hurry to leave it.

"How did you know I was here?"

"I'm ex-Search and Rescue: I know a thing or two about finding people." Her grandpa took out his hanky to blow his nose. "Pete said that Dr Cuthbertson gave the injured lady four stitches to her head. Other than being a bit shaken, she was fine. Her daughter's taken her home now." He glanced at his granddaughter. "I hear you helped out."

"More like got in everyone's way, according to Dad." Clova's voice was flat.

"Rescues set his nerves on edge. Understandable under the circumstances."

Clova couldn't keep it in any longer. "All I do is make him angry."

Grandpa sighed. "Your dad is coming to terms with the responsibility of being a single parent and the sole owner of a hotel."

"I'm not that difficult to look after."

"That's true. I once cared for an owl that couldn't fly. Now that was hard work."

Clova scowled at him.

Her grandpa cleared his throat. "When I lost your grandmother, I lost myself a bit too."

Clova didn't have a clue what he was talking about so she continued to stare at him.

Grandpa didn't want to tell her how devastated he'd

been or how his whole world had fallen apart. He paused for a moment or two, thinking about how to better explain himself in a way Clova would understand. "Male hummingbirds head off into the woods when they moult. This means they lose all their colourful plumage and without it they become vulnerable and exposed: a shadow of their former selves. And they don't want others seeing them this way because they've changed beyond all recognition. They'll only emerge from the trees when their feathers have fully grown back, and they feel just like their old selves again. It's the same for your dad. He's not at his best at the moment. He needs some time to hide away so he can heal. But he'll be back to his old self when he's ready."

"When will that be?" said Clova, hoping it would be tomorrow. Or at the very least, the end of the week.

Her grandpa shrugged. "I don't know. I doubt very much your dad does either. But I'm here for you for as long as I'm needed." He could see her face relax. The tension left her shoulders and she lowered them. He watched her anger evaporate like rainwater when it's touched by sunlight.

Clova was relieved the fighting between her and her

dad wasn't going to scare off Grandpa that easily. And that there would come a time when her dad would be less of a stranger to her. "Did you really look after an owl that couldn't fly?"

"I named him Twit for flying into the side of a barn in pursuit of a mouse. He broke both his wings."

"What happened to him?"

"Once nursed back to health, he went on to lead a long and happy life at the owl sanctuary."

Clova poked at a circular growth on the branch. It was a little smaller in size than a golf ball.

"Do you know what that is?" asked Grandpa.

She shook her head.

"That is called a gall. It's caused by the gall wasp which lays its eggs under the bark of the tree. The grubs give off chemicals that actually cause the tree to grow around them so they're protected in their own private chamber until they're ready to hatch as gall wasps."

Clova eyed him just to make sure he wasn't kidding.

"There are over seventy different species of the wasp in the UK. And the ancient Chinese used to extract tannic acid from the galls and mix it with iron sulphate to make ink."

She shook her head. "How do you know all this?"

"Because I'm old, which means I'm ridiculously wise. And on that note, I think it's time we went home." He stretched before he started to make his way back down the tree. He landed with a groan, making twigs crackle, and straightened up. He offered up his hand to help Clova down off the last branch.

"It's OK, Grandpa. I can do it."

He smiled as she landed with the flair of a gymnast dismounting from a beam. She loved how springy the ground was when it was covered in vibrant green moss, twigs, old pine needles that had turned burnt orange and small pine cones. It felt so soft, it was as if they were walking over knitted wool.

"We'd better make haste," said Grandpa, speeding up.

"Because Dad will be worried about us?"

"Because he's on dinner duty tonight and has probably set off every smoke alarm in the place by now."

Her grandpa strode off up ahead. She followed on behind, careful to walk in his footsteps.

CHAPTER 7

Clova opened all the windows in the dining room to cool the place down. It wasn't often the sky was as blue as the feathers on a jay's wings and completely cloudless. Clova could feel in her bones that today was going to be a good day with Tatty.

Mr and Mrs Paton argued about which walking route they were going to take and then sulked behind their maps when they couldn't reach a decision. Grandpa, used to keeping the peace, pointed out a third possible option that put the smiles back on their faces.

The young couple from Room 1 discovered their

teething ring did nothing to stop their crimson-cheeked baby from crying. Grandpa had whispered to Clova if they dipped it in whisky the baby would soon settle. Clova made her grandpa swear to keep that suggestion to himself.

Grandpa was in a good mood because he had the afternoon off and had arranged to go walking with a friend. After her chores, when she had asked him if she could get some fresh air, he had nodded. The Search and Rescue team were meeting at the Drovers in the afternoon as they had a fundraising event to plan, but they were more than happy to help themselves to tea and coffee. Grandpa suggested she leave a note for her dad and reminded her to be back in good time for her *surprise*. Clova rolled her eyes. Last night, her dad had actually apologized for being so short-tempered with her. He promised he'd make it up with a surprise he'd planned at two p.m. today. She wasn't holding her breath.

Clova had made real progress with Tatty and was keen to see him as soon as possible. As she hurried out of the hotel, the moors were lit bright by the rippling lochans flashing in the sunlight. The base of the mountain glowed a lush green. The grey rock face of Ben Attrin, with its ridges, shimmered in the heat. Surrounded by rare alpine plants, a cairn sat on the peak of the mountain, marking its highest point. The view from the top, on such a clear day, would be spectacular. To the right, was the imposing Ben Lore and to the left, were the seven craggy munros of Ben Lovarnach. Behind Ben Attrin was Loch Glenstrome, which Grandpa swore was home to the biggest, smartest trout in Scotland. Although Clova suspected this was a "fisherman's tale" to be taken with a pinch of salt. With such a diverse range of landscapes to explore, it was little wonder so many nature enthusiasts, ramblers, munro baggers, orienteers, mountain bikers, fishing enthusiasts and climbers stayed at the hotel.

High above Ben Attrin, Clova spotted the buzzards wheeling in circles as they hitched lifts on the thermals. She made her way across the field. Grasshoppers sounded like miniature sprinkler systems and then pinged out of her way on to stems of cow parsley. Crows spread their wings out and sunned themselves with their beaks open. Indignant at being caught, they hastily closed their wings, cawing, dry-throated, as they flapped away. Her mum would have loved a day like today. At the first opportunity, she would have escaped from the hotel into the wilds – and, later on, regaled Clova and her dad with tales of buzzards swooping down on their prey or how she'd sifted through owl pellets to see what they'd eaten. A sadness swept through Clova, and for a second everything around her dulled. Grandpa once said if you were feeling down – it was better to stop looking inwards, but instead, to look all around you.

Clova raised her eyes up. The sheep hugged the cool earthen embankments that were cabled with the intricate networks of tree roots. The air was filled with the smell of hot grass; hundreds of insects zoomed about. Clova stopped at a trickling burn to peer into it. Long green weeds undulated under the surface like a swimmer's hair. Electric blue dragonflies patrolled the banks, their bodies as iridescent as neon signs. Tempting as it was to stick her feet in the cool water, Clova didn't linger. There was a collie not so very far away that she was desperate to see.

When she arrived at the barn, Tatty had slipped behind the crates again. Clova wasn't at all surprised because in her excitement at seeing him she'd completely forgotten to approach quietly.

"Hi, Tatty!" she said. "It's me." She noticed his water bowl was nearly empty. She carried it over to the tap, filling it to the brim. On her return, a ball shot out from the gap behind the crates and rolled towards her. It came to a stop at her feet. Clova put the bowl down, water slopping over the sides of it. She picked the ball up.

It was the one she'd given Tatty yesterday!

She heard the noise of a chain scraping against wood and looked up. Tatty had come out from behind the crates. His black nose wiggled as he scented the air. A smile spread across her lips. "So, you like the ball, huh?"

Tatty lowered his head and his ears flopped forward. He licked his lips and didn't take his eye off it for a second. Clova threw the ball with too much force. It hurtled at speed towards the dog, ricocheted off the side of a crate, and smacked into a metal bar with a bang, which sent Tatty scarpering. Even the sparrows twittered in fright as it rebounded back towards her. She scooped it up and cursed her clumsiness under her breath. She placed some treats by the crates, before moving away. It didn't take long before Tatty ventured back out. He devoured the treats and studied her with interest.

Clova crouched down and, this time, threw the ball gently. Tatty's mouth fell open as he anticipated it reaching him. He pounced and grabbed it. Pleased with himself, he trotted back to the crates, chewing the ball, which squeaked. Clova tilted back her head and laughed. Never in a million years would she have believed quiet, shy, retiring Tatty could be like this. He dropped the ball and it bounced towards Clova. She snatched it up and then rolled it over to Tatty, who caught it in one swift movement and made the ball squeak six times in quick succession. Without warning, he padded over beside Clova and stretched out with the ball held between his paws. Keeping an eye on her the whole time, he busied himself plucking the woolly fibres off it.

Clova sat beside him, hardly daring to breathe. His tail swished backwards and forwards in the straw. Part of her wanted time to stop so she could stay like this for ever. As much as she was reluctant to move a muscle, she knew sitting still wasn't going to help Tatty. She needed to be walking around so he could get used to her presence. When she rose to her feet, Tatty left the ball and scurried over to the crates.

"You're OK," she assured him. As she turned, she caught sight of something draped over the gate on one of the animal pens. Clova was astonished to see it was a dog's lead. When she picked it up, Tatty stopped to stretch and then shook himself. Rannoch did exactly the same thing when he knew he was going for a walk. Tatty was excited!

Clova checked her watch. It was only twelve fifty p.m. She was certain there would be enough time to take Tatty out and be back at the Drovers for two p.m. She knew her dad was trying to make up for the way he'd spoken to her, but she'd far rather be with Tatty.

She stuck her head outside the barn. Mrs Cairncross's car wasn't around. Clova felt certain Mrs Cairncross would be pleased Tatty trusted her enough to let her exercise him. Besides, Clova had walked Rannoch heaps of times.

She took off her jumper and tied it around her waist. Clova approached Tatty, held out a treat and called his name. When he went to eat it, she unfastened the chain from his collar and clipped the lead on. Tatty aimed straight for the barn door, dragging Clova behind him. Even though he was medium sized with a slender body, he was way stronger than she'd anticipated. He galloped past the chicken coop, which sent the hens flying in a cacophony of clucks, and shot down the path leading to the fields. The dog clearly knew where he wanted to go.

She held on to the lead for dear life as they crossed the road, which thankfully was empty, and stumbled down the other side of the embankment. When Tatty saw the burn, there was no stopping him. He charged through the grass and launched himself into it, pulling Clova to the edge of the bank. He took a long drink of water. A toad appeared from nowhere and crawled towards Tatty. The dog bowed and leapt back, wagging his tail, not quite sure of the creature. Clova laughed as the toad bounced away as fast as it could to hide amongst a clump of reeds.

Without warning, Tatty gave his coat a shake, soaking her. As she wiped her face, he ran up the other side of the bank, tugging the lead. Her foot slipped and she lost her balance, falling into the burn. Tatty launched himself down the bank towards her with his ears up. He stared at her as if she had two heads. Clova struggled to her feet. Her jumper was soaked and her jeans felt a million times heavier. Water dripped everywhere.

Tatty proceeded to yank her through the tall grass. Seeds stuck to his coat and her jeans. Clova narrowly missed stepping on a giant black glistening slug that could have been mistaken for a liquorish stick. Tatty's ears flapped in the wind as they skirted past the sheep, who thundered off to the far side of the field. The dog paid no attention to them whatsoever, preferring to fling himself headlong into the undergrowth. It was crammed with thistles and nettles that stung and scratched Clova's hand. She could detect the scent of foxes: a mixture of musk, treacle and dog wee. Tatty emerged covered in burrs and tugged her towards some flowers filled with butterflies, puffing like a steam train. Keen to get closer, he nearly wrenched her arm from her socket. Crashing through the flowers, Tatty released a cloud of Painted Ladies into the sky. Clova watched, enchanted, until the collie decided it was time to take off again. Gritting her teeth, she decided to run with him. He'd been stuck on a chain for too long. No wonder he was acting so erratically. She understood that glint in his eyes was the joy of being free outdoors. It was a new world full of smells, colours, textures, excitement and fun.

Clova picked up her speed until the pair of them were tearing through the field. At the top of it was a line of trees, which she was confident would slow Tatty down. Focusing on them, she didn't notice the exposed roots, grey as old bones, that criss-crossed the ground. Her foot caught on one of them and Clova stumbled forward. Putting her hands out to break her fall, she let go of the lead. She winced at the pain in her knee as she hit the ground. Quick as a flash, she lunged to grab the lead. Tatty bombed away from her, gleeful. Now he could go wherever he pleased. He zoomed in circles around her, the lead trailing behind him. Each time he passed her, she attempted to slam her hand down on it. For the first time, Tatty's tail was straight up in the air and wagged. Clova sat up, her wet jeans covered in grass stains and a dusting of bright yellow buttercup pollen for good measure. She noticed she'd lost her jumper. It must have fallen off somewhere along the way. This was not quite how she'd imagined their walk would go. Whenever she'd been out with Rannoch, it had been nowhere near as chaotic or stressful as this.

Clova staggered to her feet. It was roasting in the sun. Sweat beaded on her forehead and pooled at the base of her back. Her chest tightened. What if she couldn't catch Tatty? Mrs Cairncross's words echoed around her head. *"Malachy Bain said the collie was a runner."*

Tatty disappeared off behind a tree.

What if he escaped into the next field? Mrs Cairncross had told her it was Malachy Bain's farm. A sign had been hammered into the ground. Written on it in red lettering was: *PRIVATE. NO TRESPASSING.*

Tatty could be in danger of being shot!

If Clova wanted to avoid a disaster, she would have to think fast.

She hurried towards the trees. Tatty stood, panting, next to the fence bordering Malachy Bain's land. Hopefully, the wire would prevent him from going through, and she'd be able to get hold of the lead. Clova jogged towards him. She shouted his name. Tatty's body language changed immediately. Gone was the happy, carefree dog. His tail lowered, he paced backwards and forwards, nervously. Before she could stop him, he slipped under the wire. Clova shouted Tatty's name. A couple of magpies, hiding in the long grass, flew away, rattling an alarm call. She sprinted towards the fence and climbed through it. By this time, Tatty was halfway down Malachy Bain's field, his lead trailing after him. She checked to see if there were any sheep. To her horror, she noticed some huddling together in the bottom right-hand corner. They had spotted the dog and were bleating, frightened. A stitch stabbed her side. Clova's mind went into a spin of all the horrible things that could happen. She stared wide-eyed in a panic. There was a ringing in her ears.

Tatty was in danger.

What she saw next made her blood run cold. The figure of a man approached the fence at the bottom of the field.

Tatty had halted now that she wasn't pursuing him. He stood panting. His ears swivelled, and then he turned to look at the man. As if caught in headlights, Tatty stood stock still, trembling. To see him like this was heart-breaking. Clova strode towards Tatty. Her eyes flicked up. She spotted an air rifle slung over the man's shoulder. She concentrated hard on not letting her legs buckle. It had to be Malachy Bain.

The sheep, crushed together, began to jump over each other. Tatty watched her. If Clova approached too fast, she'd drive him towards the farmer and his gun.

Without warning, Tatty moved in the direction of the sheep. Malachy Bain took his gun off his shoulder and pointed it straight at the collie. How could he do this to such a poor, defenceless creature? In a panic, Clova charged towards the farmer.

"Don't shoot!" she screamed at the top of her lungs. Tatty, hearing her shout, dropped and crouched low to the ground, terrified. She raced straight past the dog, to put herself in between him and the farmer. There was no way she'd let him hurt Tatty. She waved her hands in the air. "Don't shoot! Please! Don't!"

After what felt like a lifetime had passed, the man finally lowered the gun. His face was as weathered as his old wax jacket. His eyes were small and joyless. She could tell they didn't miss a trick. He put his foot on the lowest rung of the wire fence. It squeaked as it dipped.

"That dog is causing distress to my sheep," he said, tilting his head towards Tatty.

She drew herself up to her full height. "He's not interested in the sheep. He's just frightened."

"I lost four good ewes a couple of weeks ago. Do you know what the owner said to me? Her dog wasn't capable of harming a fly."

"I'm sorry that happened to you and your sheep, Mr Bain. That's awful."

The farmer spat on to the grass. "You're wasting your time. That collie is a liability."

"No thanks to you."

Malachy Bain took his foot off the fence. She could see his fingers turning white as he gripped the gun. "You're lucky I didn't shoot him. If I see that dog in this field again, there will be consequences. Now, get it under control, and get out of my field before I call the police."

Clova didn't want to imagine how that conversation would go with her dad.

She had to catch Tatty first. Malachy Bain's eyes bored straight through her. Clova wished the ground would open up and swallow her whole.

How could she get Tatty back without upsetting the sheep further?

What would Isla do? she thought.

A memory came to her of Isla working with Rannoch. She had treats and she'd called Rannoch to her. Clova remembered that Isla didn't run around after Rannoch. In fact, she had done quite the opposite, and walked away from him. Anything was worth a try.

Clova brought the last treat out of her pocket, cursing that she hadn't brought more with her. Ignoring Malachy Bain, she called the dog's name, careful to keep the fear out of her voice.

"Here, Tatty!"

Tatty's ears pricked up. Clova fought the urge to approach him. It would only drive him further towards the sheep. Instead, she backed off. Tatty glanced in the direction of farmer and then the sheep, weighing up his options. She could see that he wasn't sure what to do. Just as she was certain he was going to bolt, he trotted towards her. Clova's heart banged inside her chest, hard. She remembered Isla telling her that her mum thought she might follow in her grandpa's footsteps by training dogs. This steadied her nerves and gave her some confidence. Clova continued to walk away from Tatty, and called to him again. He sniffed the air and licked his lips. Tatty kept on going until he was right in front of her. As she lowered her hand, he took the treat from her gently. In one swift movement, she swooped down for the lead and praised him. The collie seemed less than impressed. He panted, his eyes fixed on the fields, the moors and the mountain.

Clova looked back at the farmer. He had gone. Having lost all track of time, she checked her watch. She only had fifteen minutes to deliver Tatty to the farm and make it back to the Drovers on time! Tired from his adventure, Tatty no longer strained on the lead. They set off at speed, finally heading in the direction of Stoneburn Farm.

As they were nearing the burn, Tatty pulled her over to the left. She tried to correct him, but he leant his body away from her and insisted on going in that direction. Sighing, she gave in. He glued his nose to the ground and sniffed it until he reached a patch of tall grass. There he stopped and snuffled at something. Clova was amazed to see her jumper lying there. She snatched it up, wrung it out, and re-tied it around her waist. Tatty guided them back to the farm. With no time to catch her breath, Clova sped off towards the Drovers.

CHAPTER 8

Clova made quite the entrance, flying through the door to the hotel bar. In the commotion, Bob Cram, one of the locals, spilled his drink.

Clova's dad put down the glass he was drying. He clocked her damp, grass-stained jeans, not-so-white-top and wild hair.

"You look like you've been dragged through the fields," he commented.

She shrugged. "Threw myself into my chores today."

"You threw yourself into something, all right," he said.

If her dad knew what had happened this afternoon,

he'd be furious. Even Clova couldn't quite believe she'd stood between Tatty and an angry farmer with a gun. The thought made her shiver. Pushing it out of her mind, she peered around the bar to see if she could spot what her surprise was.

The door swung open. In walked Sally with her mum. Clova wondered what on earth they were doing at the hotel. Her stomach lurched as it dawned on her that Sally must be her surprise. She had hoped it might be something good like joining Isla and Rannoch for a walk after their Search and Rescue meeting. Or a trip to the safari park she loved with her dad. They hadn't been anywhere nice together since Mum had died. It dawned on Clova that all of this paled in comparison to being with Tatty.

"Hullo, Sally! How are you?" said her dad, brightening up his voice.

Her dad had no clue Sally and her weren't exactly the best of friends any more.

Sally's mum nudged her forward. "I'm fine thanks, Mr McFarlane," she said without any enthusiasm. She wasn't exactly ecstatic to be here either.

Clova gawped at Sally. Her hair was perfectly styled

and highlighted, she had glitter gel nails and a brand new pair of Converse.

"Well, isn't this nice? It's been a while. The last time we were here it was..." Sally's mum stopped talking.

Clova knew the last time they had been at the Drovers was for her mum's funeral.

"... Was far too long ago – isn't that right?" Sally's mum said. Her eyes drifted over Clova's unkempt hair and mucky jeans. She dropped her gaze.

"Clova will enjoy the company of someone her own age, for a change," said her dad.

"Was that the Search and Rescue team I saw?" asked Sally's mum.

"They're planning a fundraiser in a couple of weeks. It's going to be here and we're hoping for a good turnout. You'd be very welcome to come along," said Clova's dad.

"We would love that. Anything to show our support. It's always comforting to know help is at hand should you ever need it. Right, I'd better get going," said Sally's mum. "This one's granny is coming to tea and the cupboards are bare. I'll be back to collect her in an hour."

She approached Clova's dad and clasped his hand in her own. The trinkets on her bracelet scraped against the wooden surface of the bar. She dropped her voice. "If you ever need me to take her shopping for … *girl's things* … she'd be more than welcome to join Sally and me."

Clova wasn't sure where to look.

Her dad slid his hand out of her grip. "We manage just fine – thanks all the same."

"Of course you do. The offer is always there if you change your mind," she said, as she fished her car keys out of her denim jacket pocket. "Bye, girls. Have fun." She waved at them on her way out. After she'd gone, the scent of her perfume lingered in the air.

Her dad leant over the bar. "Would you ladies like something to drink?"

Clova bristled. Of all the people to be stuck with. Some surprise this was. Sally being here was bad enough. But the thought of her dad listening in on their conversation made everything a million times worse.

"Is it OK if we go out?" asked Clova. "We'll stick close by," she added quickly.

Her dad straightened up. He grabbed two cans of

cola and a couple of bags of crisps. He passed them over to the girls. Sally put them in her Vans rucksack.

"Make sure you're back in an hour," said her dad, before he served a customer.

Clova led the way into the reception. "What do you want to do?"

"Dunno. Watch something on YouTube?" Sally suggested, taking her phone out from her pocket.

"The reception out here can be a bit dodgy. How about we go down to the river? We can cool off if it gets too hot."

Sally pulled a face.

Clova would far rather be with Tatty. She wondered if he'd be curled up sleeping, tired out after their adventure. Or pacing up and down, wishing he was free to run where he pleased.

The girls sauntered across the car park towards a steep bank of long grass, which they made their way down. Sally shouted out and flapped her hand. She'd been stung by nettles.

"Are you OK?" asked Clova.

Sally didn't even bother to answer, but stomped on ahead. Now she definitely didn't want to be here.

Clova took a deep breath. She wished she could enter the water, lie back and let the river carry her off, far away downstream. When they reached the bank, a tiny kingfisher flashed past them, its bright blue and orange feathers a shock of colour against the muted greens of the plants and trees. By the time Sally had looked in the right direction, the bird had vanished.

The girls took their shoes off, rolled up their jeans, and waded over to flat grey slabs of hot rock. It was hard to believe only a couple of days ago the river was so high it would have been impossible to cross.

Sally took her phone out and tutted. "I'd forgotten how rotten the signal is here."

Clova waved up at the family from Room 1, who were on the bridge taking pictures of the views, their baby now fast asleep. Sally scowled at them.

There was a time when Clova and Sally were inseparable. Sometimes they could tell what the other was thinking just by the arch of an eyebrow or a twitch of the mouth. Whenever they'd had sleepovers at each other's homes, they'd chatter and laugh so much that they always got into trouble for staying up late and being too noisy. Clova was an only child but Sally gave her a glimpse of what it might be like to have a sister, which she had loved. She had always admired Sally's fearlessness and had wanted to be more like her. Now, it was like they were perfect strangers. Clova didn't even know what to say.

Sally swatted away a fly and muttered under her breath. She fished around in her rucksack and brought out the drinks and crisps. Sally cracked open her can and took a long swig from it.

Clova patted her head, felt something that shouldn't be there and pulled a leaf out. "I like your shoes," she said.

"Went on a shopping trip with my mum to Edinburgh. She took me to Nando's for lunch."

It hit Clova like a steam train that she would never be able to go for lunch with her mum again. She fought to catch her breath.

Sally tucked her hair behind her ear and pointed to a gold stud. "I managed to persuade Mum to let me get my ears pierced. It hurt loads, but it was worth it."

Clova shot her a glance. They'd made a promise that they'd get their ears pierced, together. Sally had always said she'd make Clova laugh at the exact moment her ears were being done, so she wouldn't feel the pain. But Sally had forgotten all about that. And she clearly hadn't noticed Clova had gone quiet. It had even escaped her to ask Clova how she'd been. Or to mention her mum. Eventually, Sally stopped talking about herself and lay down, using her rucksack as a makeshift pillow. She played some music on her phone and waved her arms and legs around as she danced to it, lying flat.

A heron landed near them in search of its dinner. After a while, the music sounded tinny as the battery on Sally's phone ran low. Sally yawned, switched it off, and closed her eyes.

Clova checked her phone, relieved Sally's mum would be here for her soon. Sitting next to somebody you had no clue what to say to was exhausting.

A breeze blew in, its breath puckering the surface of the river. Clova watched as sunlight bursts swarmed over the water's surface as if some kind of Disney magic was taking place. She stuck her toes in the river, enjoying the jolt of the water's coldness that woke up every nerve in her body. She could make out the shapes of tiny fish wriggling as they swam against the current.

Her mind drifted off to falling in the burn earlier. And how Tatty had run on to Malachy Bain's land. What a close shave that had been! She needed a proper plan of action in place. She watched the sparkles on the water a while longer. That's when it came to her: she would start training Tatty with some basic commands. Every time she visited, she could do some work with him in the barn. And she'd make sure they never ventured near Malachy Bain's field again.

Sally had opened one eye. "You're *lucky* living in a hotel. You have lots of different people staying all of the time and I bet they're really interesting."

Clova didn't see the point in bringing up that the place wasn't the same without her mum there. It felt less like a home. It was filled with strangers, who would be there for a few days, before they returned to their normal lives. Something she could never do. Clova doubted Sally would understand any of this. Or care.

"Do you miss being out of town? Like, does it get boring?" Sally wiggled her toes.

Clova remembered Malachy Bain with his gun pointed at Tatty. And running through the fields at top speed with the collie. She propped herself up on her elbows, wanting to tell Sally about Tatty. But she stopped herself. Things had changed between them. There was no point in sharing a secret with someone who wasn't really her friend any more. She pushed all thoughts of Tatty from her mind. "There's always something happening here. I've been helping out the Search and Rescue team a bit. And I go for walks. The mountain, woods and moors are kind of like my back garden."

Sally wrinkled up her nose. "You'd go near that mountain?"

Clova sat up, brushing her hands together. "Why wouldn't I?"

Sally looked astounded. "Because it killed your mum."

The words felt like daggers in Clova's heart. "The mountain didn't kill Mum. The weather conditions did. My mum loved everything about Ben Attrin. So I won't stay away from it. In fact, I hope one day I'll be part of a team that saves lives on it too."

"Are you for real? Have you got a death wish or something?"

"You're just as bad as my dad." Clova scrambled

to her feet. She landed in the water with a splash and waded through it. She grabbed her shoes and hopped into them, small stones sticking to her bare soles. With Sally hot on her heels, she ran up the embankment and crossed the car park as Sally's mum pulled up. Sally appeared behind Clova, red-faced, clutching on to her rucksack and phone.

Sally coming there had been a mistake, but Clova didn't want to cause a scene. She saw her half-smile reflected in Sally's mum's sunglasses.

"Hi, girls! Did you have a good time?" asked Sally's mum.

Clova nodded.

"Oh, that's great. I'm glad Sally was good company. I told her you'd need cheering up."

Sally passed around the front of the car and climbed in without saying a word.

"You caught the sun, Sal." Her mum said as Sally fastened her seatbelt with a face like thunder. "Hopefully we can return the favour and you'll come to ours next time?"

"Great!" Clova's toes curled up inside her shoes.

Sally looked away.

Clova stepped back and waved at Sally's mum as they left. She puffed air out of her mouth as the car disappeared over the bridge. Clova slunk back into the hotel. She couldn't possibly tell her dad she'd had a rotten time. He'd be so disappointed after going to the trouble of phoning Sally's mum.

She stuck her head around the dining-room door but the Search and Rescue meeting had finished. Everyone had left.

Clova traipsed into the kitchen. Grandpa was standing at the sink peeling potatoes. "There you are!" he said.

"Did you know my surprise was Sally?"

"I may have had an inkling." He put the peeler down and faced her. He could see his granddaughter appeared more troubled than carefree. "Did you have a good time?"

She got some apple juice from the fridge and poured herself a glass. "Sally spoke about herself. A. Lot." Clova sat down at the table. "She never once asked how I was."

"Did you tell her?"

"Didn't see the point."

“Well, how can she possibly know if you don’t say a thing?”

Clova shrugged. “She has highlights and gel nails.”

“That sounds painful.” Her grandpa dried his hands and sat opposite her. “I know today can’t have been easy, Clova. But you should let her know how you’re feeling and not bottle it up. That’s not good for anyone. If you show her you’re comfortable talking about your mum, then she’ll realize it’s OK for her to talk about her too.”

Clova rested her head in her hands.

“Sally still has her mum, so can’t begin to imagine what life might be like without her. It’s possibly a bit too scary to put herself in your shoes.”

What he said made sense. The fact she still had her mum wasn’t exactly Sally’s fault. Clova looked at him. “She can’t understand why I still like Ben Attrin after what happened.”

“You’ve been raised to love it. You have a connection to it through here and here.” He tapped his head lightly and then his heart. “Same as your mother.”

The landslide of emotions slipping into the pit of her stomach stopped. For the first time today it felt as though her head wasn't all over the place.

"I say give Sally another chance and talk to her this time. If it doesn't work out then at least you know you tried. Friends don't have to be for ever, Clova. Sometimes the right person appears at the right time for you, and then you go your separate ways so you can let new people into your life. You mustn't worry so much."

"You mean, I shouldn't worry as much as Dad."

"I wouldn't recommend it."

Clova leant forward to nudge her Grandpa's arm affectionately. "Thanks."

"Anytime – apart from when I'm busy."

Clova smiled. "Did you have a good afternoon?"

Her grandpa leapt up and continued peeling the potatoes. "It was wonderful seeing Sandy again. He's a walking encyclopaedia when it comes to plants and their medicinal qualities. He's in his seventies and he's a spring in his step of someone in their forties."

"Is that because he knows all the right plants to eat?"

"It's because he always carries a hip-flask with him wherever he goes."

Clova burst out laughing for what felt like the first

time that day.

Her grandpa placed the spuds in a pan of boiling water. Nothing made him happier than seeing the weight his granddaughter carried around with her lift. Her face could light up an entire room when she let go of her troubles. Just the same way her mum could. The familiar pain of his daughter's loss swept through him and for a moment or two he became swamped by his grief.

"Need help with dinner?" asked Clova, wondering why he'd suddenly gone quiet.

"Everything is under control," he said, regaining his composure. " Except for the fridge. I've never seen so many eggs. We're going to have to live off omelette, toad in the hole and quiche for the rest of our lives. Do you know anything about this?"

Clova's eyes widened a touch. She'd need to start refusing the eggs from Mrs Cairncross otherwise Grandpa would find out she'd been going to Stoneburn Farm every day. "Don't know a thing about it." Clova could feel a heat creeping across her cheeks.

Her grandpa added salt to the boiling water. "Before I forget, these are for you." He pushed a folder that was lying on the kitchen table towards her.

She opened it. Inside was a pile of laminated sheets. Each one tackling a different aspect on Search and Rescue training for dogs. Clova studied them for a while and then scooped the lot up, clutching them to her. This was exactly what she needed to help Tatty.

"They're cards from the course I used to run. Ignore the more advanced techniques, but if you rootle around you'll find some of the basic commands in there," said her grandpa with a sniff.

Clova stared at him. She couldn't help it. Her eyes watered because she was so over the moon. "Are you sure?"

"I've got copies, Clova, so this set is yours."

Grandpa brought some sausages out the oven and placed the hot tray on top of the cooker. "I thought it might be something you'd like to read up on after all the questions you've been asking recently."

Clova's dad walked into the kitchen.

"Look, Dad! Grandpa gave me some notes on how to train a dog!"

"Is this for a project?" he asked, taken aback. He wasn't used to Clova being quite so pleased to see him.

He leant against the kitchen unit.

"I'm just really interested in it."

Her dad reached over to put the salt and pepper on the table. She held her breath, waiting to see if he'd find a way to disapprove of the notes. He surprised her.

"Did you enjoy your day?"

"It's been great, thanks, Dad."

As Grandpa started to dish up their dinner, he watched his son-in-law and granddaughter smile and chat to each other, the way they used to. Something that hadn't happened in a long time.

"You wouldn't happen to know why we've a fridge stuffed full of eggs would you, Jim?" said Grandpa.

"You've got me there, Archie," Clova's dad replied, scratching his stubble.

"It appears we have an egg fairy in our midst," said Grandpa, pouring hot gravy over the sausages.

CHAPTER 9

Clova had pinned the cards all over her bedroom wall. Each one had photos and illustrations of dogs doing step-by-step training exercises. Whether she was lying in bed or sitting on her beanbag chair or at her desk, she could focus on a different technique until she had memorized all the basics.

For the last two weeks, she'd become an expert at sneaking out when her dad was still asleep after the nightshift and her grandpa was knee-deep in sorting out bookings for the hotel or attending meetings for the upcoming Search and Rescue Fundraising event.

By leaving notes and being fast to answer calls or reply to texts, her dad slowly began to trust her more. Soon her time with Tatty was all she thought about. It was the reason she leapt out of bed in the morning with a lightness in her step and why she stayed awake late into the night, excited at all the adventures they could have together.

At first, the training hadn't gone well at all. Tatty had sat up on a crate, refused to move and eyed her warily. Or he'd walked off to find something far more interesting to sniff at in amongst the stalls or machinery. As soon as she produced some treats, Tatty began to pay attention to her, his head tilting to one side when she spoke to him.

The more time she spent time with him, the more Clova began to notice how expressive he was. She could tell how he was feeling by the angle of his ears. If they were pinned back, he was alarmed. If they were raised, he was trying to figure out what was going on. And if they were neither raised nor pinned back, Tatty was at ease. If he was anxious, he'd pace up and down and show the whites of his eyes. But when he was relaxed, he'd sit with his eyes half closed as if he was about to fall asleep. If he had no idea what she was asking of him, he'd make a puffing noise, shuffle backwards away from her and lie down with his head on his paws. When he was being cheeky he'd cuff her hand with a paw, in the hope she'd open her fingers and give him the treat – without him having to do any work for it. When he was bored he'd chew on the lead. And when he wanted to get her attention he'd bump the back of her leg with his nose, which always made her chuckle.

Day by day, Clova watched as he came out of his shell. Every afternoon, Tatty waited for her, his tail sweeping backwards and forwards in the straw. He'd nudge his ball towards her, and she'd throw it in the air for him to leap up and catch. Then he'd be at her coat pockets to check for treats. If Clova went to stroke him, he'd jump back, unsure. Clova resigned herself to being patient. Tatty may never be comfortable with his ears being rubbed, his back being scratched or his belly being tickled. Not all dogs were.

Much to her surprise, after a million false starts, he began coming to her when she called his name. Clova knew it was because Tatty loved a tasty treat.

And that they were inside the barn, which had very few distractions.

Today, though, would be a different matter because it'd be the first time she'd attempted to train with Tatty outdoors. Clova had spied a small paddock behind the house at Stoneburn Farm. It would be perfect as it had walls and a gate. There was no way he'd escape on to Malachy Bain's field again. Not on her watch.

Putting the lead on Tatty, they left the barn at the same speed a husky pulls a sled. They shot past the farmhouse and entered the field; Tatty beside himself with excitement because he'd never explored it before. Clova shut the gate behind them and swapped Tatty's lead with a spare long-line of Rannoch's that Isla kept at the Drovers. It was several metres longer than an ordinary leash. Although Tatty was free to go wherever he pleased, she could easily pick it up to guide him if she needed. The lead trailed behind him as he ran around sniffing different scents and piddling on clumps of thistles.

Clova cracked her knuckles, took a breath and readied herself.

"Tatty. Come!"

Tatty stopped chewing on the grass and stared at her. An ear flopped down over his eye. Clova had seen Isla working with the long-line before. She picked up the leash, took up the slack and gave it a gentle tug as she called his name again. He ran towards her. Just as she was about to praise him, he veered off to sniff a dried out old sheep poop.

"Really, Tatty?" Clova laughed. "Sheep poop is more interesting than me? We'll see about that." Her eyes moved skywards as she thought about a new tactic to try. Tatty bounded over to a patch of foxgloves in the corner of the field.

This time she halved the distance between them. Clova called Tatty's name again and gave the leash a small tug. Tatty galloped towards her and then shot straight past to follow a cabbage white butterfly around the paddock.

Clova shook her head. She would have to make herself more exciting. She took a moment and then clapped her hands together. Tatty immediately wondered what she was up to. She called his name, walked backwards away from him and waved her hands in the air to attract his attention. Tatty bounded in her direction and she cheered him on. When he reached her, she squealed with delight, crouched and gave him his reward. Then she ran a victory lap around the field, whooping at the top of her voice. Tatty decided to join in and chased after her, barking. Clova heard someone laughing. Mrs Cairncross was leaning on the gate, watching the entire spectacle.

Clova skidded to a halt, mortified she'd been seen. She wondered for a split second if Malachy Bain had said anything to Mrs Cairncross about her and Tatty trespassing in his field. Her heart skipped a few beats.

"Training going well?" asked Mrs Cairncross.

Clova jogged over to the gate. "We're working on his recall."

"Looks like he's enjoying himself."

"Seemingly dogs and schoolkids have a lot in common: the more fun the class, the more they learn."

Mrs Cairncross laughed. "He has a good teacher. You're a natural at it."

Clova shrugged. "Tatty's the clever one."

Just as she said that, Tatty went over to the sheep poop and took a nibble of it. He threw himself down and rubbed his ear with his paw. Clova thought back to the Tatty who had hidden from her behind the wooden crates. There was a still a long way to go with him yet, but they'd made good progress now he was relaxed in her company.

"I've good news." From the shine in her eyes, Clova knew it must be something big.

"I was chatting to a friend of mine and, quite by chance, they mentioned they're looking for a dog. They're raising a young family and have a large garden, which is fenced. They're camping enthusiasts and would love a dog to join them on their trips." Mrs Cairncross grinned. "I think Tatty would be perfect."

"Oh, that's..." Clova didn't finish her sentence.

"It's what we wanted for him."

"Do you think he's ready?" asked Clova. "He's OK with you and me because he knows us. He might be jittery with them."

"I've mentioned Tatty's had a difficult start and that he's nervous. I've also made it clear he needs lots of patience, understanding and training. But, Clova, this might be the best opportunity for a dog like him. He deserves a home of his own and a family to belong to."

Clova let her breath out. Mrs Cairncross was right.

Tatty couldn't stay chained up in a draughty barn for ever. It wasn't fair. And with a family, he'd have lots of people to love him and make a fuss of him. Yet, something was stopping her being pleased for Tatty. She could feel her heart sinking all the way down into her boots.

Mrs Cairncross stuck her hands in her pockets. "You've grown fond of him."

Clova watched Tatty nibble on his paw and then chew on a piece of grass. She realized she loved him more than anything else in the world. "I never expected a thing from him and every day he surprises me."

Mrs Cairncross nodded. "I'll have a word with the family. I dare say they will be more than happy for you to visit him, if you want?"

Clova dropped her gaze and fought hard not to let her eyes well up. She could never tell her dad about Tatty, because he'd find out she'd been lying to him. He'd never trust her again. Once Tatty left, the dog would be out of her life for good.

"I doubt I'd have the time once school starts – with the hotel and everything."

Mrs Cairncross hesitated. "I'll mention it to them anyway, in case you change your mind. One last thing before I go: I know the Drovers is hosting the Search and Rescue fundraiser tomorrow and was wondering if you'd need some extra eggs?"

"*No!* Thank you, Mrs Cairncross, we have plenty."

Mrs Cairncross nodded. "By the way, you've jam on your face." She began to walk back to the farmhouse.

Clova wiped her mouth. "When are they coming for Tatty?"

"Tomorrow at three p.m." Mrs Cairncross waved before she disappeared out of sight.

Clova sat on the ground, feeling as though the stuffing had been knocked out of her. It was hard to get her head around losing Tatty. Life would be unimaginable without him. When she was with the collie, she was always so happy. Panic chewed its way through her stomach at the thought of losing him.

Tatty yawned and stretched. He picked up a stick and trotted over to where Clova was, sniffed at her shoe and then her knee. He dropped the stick on her lap and settled beside her.

"Are you trying to cheer me up by any chance?"

Tatty's ears swivelled but his eyes focused on Ben Attrin.

Together, they watched as the clouds drifted over the mountain. His ears rose up as a curlew flew past. She marvelled at the swallows as they twisted across the vast blue of the sky. There was something about being with Tatty that made her feel settled. Content. Complete again. Without thinking, she put her hand out to stroke the fur on the back of his neck. Tatty leant in. Clova wanted to stay like this for ever.

CHAPTER 10

The light blinded Clova as someone entered her room. After blinking twice she could see it was Grandpa. He was glancing around at all the dog training cards she'd stuck up on the walls.

"Morning, Clova."

She sat up. Her sheets were tangled. There was a glimmer of a familiar feeling that grazed her heart. Then it came back to her. Tatty would be leaving today.

"Time to get up. Word about town is the turnout for the Search and Rescue fundraiser is going to be good."

"What do you want me to do?" Clova yawned and stretched.

"I think it's going to be a case of us rolling up our sleeves and jumping in to help where we can."

The event would provide her with the perfect cover to slip off to say her goodbyes to Tatty. When she imagined seeing him for the last time, the back of her throat ached. "Grandpa?"

He tilted his head, waiting for her to speak.

"What do you do when you should be pleased about something good happening, but instead you feel really sad?"

"Drink whisky?"

"*Grandpaaa!*"

He sat at the end of her bed. "What you're feeling is something we all go through. Being happy for others is a mark of kindness, Clova, a quality you have in abundance."

It didn't make her feel any better about Tatty going.

He got to his feet with a groan. "Wish me luck."

"What for?"

"I'm about to wake your dad. I'm armed with coffee and a bacon roll to aid with his transition into becoming a bright-eyed and bushy-tailed morning person."

Clova smiled at her grandpa. She and Dad would be so lost without him here. Her grandpa pointed at one of the training cards which had a black-and-white photo of a cocker spaniel on it. "That was Beau. I trained her in 1998. If ever the rescue was unsuccessful, she'd go around every member of the team afterwards to make sure they were OK. She wasn't taught to, she just sensed when people were upset. Never forgot that remarkable dog." Her grandpa patted the picture and left her room.

Clova leapt out of her bed, threw on a top and jeans, and stood by the mirror. She knew Grandpa was right. She should be happy for Tatty.

Clova took a deep breath.

She could do this.

*

Behind the hotel, stalls had been set up selling baking, bric-a-brac, second-hand outdoor gear and on-the-spot animal face painting for kids. A large marquee had been put up the day before for the Search and Rescue fundraising auction. Clova took a peek inside. The set of square plastic windows behind the stage perfectly framed the mountain, which towered over the proceedings, reminding everyone why they were there – to raise money for equipment that would save lives. Every member of the team was going to put themselves up for auction in the hope they made a fortune. Pete was offering a course of rock-climbing lessons and Isla a one-to-one dog-training lesson. Plus she was going to be doing a demonstration later on with Rannoch to show everyone why he was such a superstar.

Clova busied herself ferrying chairs from the hotel to the marquee. Then she lent a hand to Jane Robertson who was setting up her pet supplies stall. Which was handy when her teacher, Miss Willow, walked past, because Clova wanted to avoid her. She ducked down and began to unpack some of Jane's boxes. She spotted a bright red tartan collar with a bone-shaped, silver name tag. She reckoned it would fit Tatty perfectly and was keen for him to have a keepsake of their time together. Clova paid for it and tucked it in her pocket next to the note she'd written for Tatty's new owners. In it she'd listed all the things he loved: playing fetch with his ball, exploring new places, piddling on fallen branches, splashing around in the water, cats, rolling in fox poop, belly rubs, hunting for treats, following scents, being talked to, drinking from puddles and being dried with a towel.

Clova didn't want him to go. She would give anything for him to stay. But she really did hope the letter would help the family settle Tatty into his new home. It was what he deserved.

As people started to arrive, it became busy. One minute she would be showing guests to their rooms and the next she'd be serving up tea, coffee and cakes on a stall. She returned a lost West Highland Terrier to a family and set out bowls of water around the place for all the thirsty dogs. She soon discovered that bombing around the place kept her mind off of having to say goodbye to Tatty.

She'd caught a glimpse of Sally in the crowds and remembered her grandpa's words about giving her another chance. Clova didn't want to fall out with her. They weren't as close as they had been, but that didn't mean they couldn't be friends. On her way to the stalls, Clova spotted Sally coming her way. As Clova smiled, Sally stuck her nose in the air and kept on walking.

Clova stopped, not believing what had just happened. People bumped into her as they jostled past.

A crowd cheered behind her. The auction had begun.

"There you are! The bar is jam-packed and your dad's running out of glasses because they're not being cleared from the tables. I've been called to the auction. Can you take care of it?" asked her grandpa.

Clova nodded. People squeezed the breath out of her as she fought her way inside the hotel. She had never seen the bar so busy. Clova spotted her dad moving like lightning. The tables were full of dirty glasses, coffee cups and cold pots of tea. She started to collect up the glasses, slotting them inside each other into a stack. As she headed for the bar, Clova saw Malachy Bain standing in the queue to order a drink. What if he told her dad about her and Tatty trespassing in his field? The glasses slipped through her fingers and smashed on the floor. The whole place fell silent. Everyone turned to stare. Clova's dad frowned at her.

She bent to pick up the glass and felt a piece cut her finger. Clova dropped it and stood. The room began to spin. It was like she was back at school again. And everyone was trying to get a glimpse of the kid whose mum had died on the mountain.

The crowd parted and Isla stepped in. "Come with me. It's time for a break," Isla shouted over to Marie to tidy up the broken glass. She took Clova by the elbow to steer her out. She opened the backdoor and yelled that they were coming through. People jumped out of their way and they entered the outhouse.

Clova let Isla examine her hand.

"No stitches required, thankfully. I'm not too good on the sewing front – unless it's the turkey at Christmas." Isla took down the first aid kit and tore open an antiseptic wipe. The wipe was cool against Clova's skin and nipped along the edges of the cut. Isla cleaned the wound and sealed it with a plaster.

"There. Good as new."

Clova looked at her phone. It was two thirty p.m. Tatty would be gone soon. Anxiety gripped her heart in a stranglehold.

Isla peered at Clova. "Are you OK?"

There was a part of Clova that couldn't face saying goodbye to Tatty. That it might be less painful just staying at the Drovers.

"I haven't eaten today," she confessed.

Isla reached into her pocket and brought out a cheese and tomato roll. "It's from Sheila's stall. Very tasty, and guaranteed to have you energized in no time."

Clova took it out of the paper bag and nibbled at it. Some chutney fell out of the roll on to her jeans. She wiped it off.

"Would you like to watch Rannoch and I doing our demonstration? You can bring what's left of your roll and sit on the sidelines."

"How long will it take?"

"Twenty minutes or so." Isla put her hands on her hips. "Hey – if anyone comes looking for you to do more chores, Rannoch will see them off."

"He'd do that?"

"He looks out for his nearest and dearest." Isla winked at her.

Clova would love to see Isla and Rannoch in action. Afterwards, it would be easy for her to slip off to Stoneburn Farm if her dad didn't come looking for her. She was bound to be in hot water with him after smashing all those glasses. He'd be angry at her for being more of a hinderance than a help. And what if Malachy Bain had said something to him?

"Are you sure everything is OK? You don't seem your usual self."

Clova's eyes swivelled to the ground. Her foot kicked at the table leg. "Mum would have loved this: everyone in the town being here, the laughter, Moira's millionaire's shortbread, and raising money for the team."

"What do you think your mum would have done for the auction?" asked Isla.

"I think she'd have suggested a guided tour of Ben Attrin. Whenever a walk was booked by hotel guests it made her happy. It gave her the chance to show off the mountain so others loved it as much as she did."

Isla nodded in agreement. "Do you know the fundraising for Search and Rescue started out as a raffle? I do believe a wonky hand-knitted woolly hat was one of the prizes. Your mum sensed it could be something bigger that involved the whole community and she was right. So we're all here because of her."

Clova polished off the last of the roll. "Thanks for patching me up."

"I'd better go and fetch the star of the show. He's having his make-up done in his trailer."

Clova laughed, knowing full well Rannoch would be in the jeep and Isla was fibbing.

"Be kind to yourself, Clova. You've been through a lot, and you're still going through a lot." Isla headed for the door.

"See you later, alligator!" piped up Clova.

"Back in a while, crocodile!" answered Isla before she left.

Clova made her way to the field where a large crowd was already gathering. She climbed through the fence for her ringside seat.

There was a ripple of applause. Clova raised her head as Rannoch bounded into the field. The Alsatian ran straight over and puffed in her face as she patted him. Isla laughed and called his name. He trotted over to Isla, not taking his eyes off his trainer once. He looked so dapper in the sunshine. Rannoch held himself in a way that showed he was well aware of his importance. Pride swelled in Clova's chest. If that had been her and Tatty, their entrance would have been more slapstick.

Clova was transfixed as Rannoch obeyed Isla's

every word. In fluid movements, he "sat", "stayed", "fetched" and "barked" on command. Isla spoke to the crowd, informing them Rannoch had more successful finds than any other dog in Scotland since he started service as a Search and Rescue dog. The Alsatian wasn't at all alarmed by the loud cheers and whistles. Isla produced a toy of Rannoch's. It was an old piece of rope that had been knotted at both ends. Isla explained that this was Rannoch's reward when he found someone. The Alsatian gripped one end of the rope and tugged. Isla, too, tugged back in a playful way. Rannoch dug his heels in, loving the game. Isla told the crowd that the rope was better than a ball on rescue missions because there was less chance it would bounce over the edge of a cliff.

Isla then made Rannoch sit. There was laughter as she took a shoe off a willing participant in the audience. She gave it to Rannoch to scent. She then positioned Rannoch so he couldn't see her, made him stay, and hid the shoe high up in a hedge on the other side of the field. Isla returned to the Alsatian and told him to "seek". Rannoch methodically sniffed his way around the field working from left to right.

Clova was fascinated and watched him with laser-like focus.

Isla explained that the scent from the shoe would come down from the hedge, hit the ground and rise up again like a rolling wave. She then explained that if Rannoch was downwind from the shoe, he'd detect the smell faster. It wasn't long before Rannoch bounded towards the hedge. He smelled his way around the base of it but didn't find anything. Being experienced, he looked up and sniffed the air, his nose hard at work again. When he was certain he'd locked on to the scent of the shoe, he barked. Isla praised Rannoch and gave him his rope toy to play with. He trotted off with it pleased as punch. The audience went wild with applause. Clova stood and clapped until her hands burned. Isla returned the shoe back to the owner and let a young boy pat the Alsatian.

Rannoch finding the hidden shoe reminded her of Tatty leading Clova to her jumper in the field.

Tatty!

She checked her watch. There was just enough time

to run over to the farm to see him.

Clova saw her chance. Isla was chatting to an elderly couple who wanted to meet Rannoch. She sidled off towards the edge of the field. Just as she was about to make her exit, she heard her name being called.

She turned to see her dad.

Clova glanced longingly in the direction of Stoneburn Farm. She couldn't miss Tatty leaving! That would break her heart.

"*Clova!* Did you not hear me calling?"

She approached her dad, slowly, trying to read him from a distance. Was this about the glasses? Or had Malachy Bain told him about Tatty?

"Come with me, young lady." Her dad couldn't have wanted to cause a scene in front of people. She followed him back to the hotel, dragging her heels. Her dad led Clova to the dining room. She couldn't bear this. She had to be with Tatty one last time.

Her eyes blazed. "Do we need to do this right now? Can't it wait?"

"No, it can't. Why didn't you tell me?" Her dad stood, hand on hips. Even his shirts were looking too big for him now. He narrowed his eyes at her.

She shrugged. "Tell you what?"

"Oh, don't start. This affects your future."

Clova frowned. She'd smashed some glasses. Not robbed a bank. Unless Malachy Bain had complained about her.

"I know things have been difficult, but can you not talk to me any more? Is that how bad things are between us? I have to hear it from Miss Willow?"

Clova shook her head slowly, confused. "Hear what?"

"That your grades have slipped. You're behind in class. And you turned down the opportunity to catch up over the summer with some extra work."

"Is that all?" Clova let out a sigh of relief.

"What's got into to you? I've agreed with Miss Willow that she'll come and help you with your schoolwork. She's confident she can get you up to speed for the start of First Year."

Clova checked the time on her phone.

"Do you have somewhere more important to be right now?" There was a flash of annoyance in her dad's voice.

Marie stuck her head around the door. "Sorry to disturb. There's a barrel that needs changing and a couple of food orders?"

Her dad gave her a look. "Don't move, Clova. I'll be back in a minute."

The room was hot and stuffy. There was a faint cloying smell of sausages, eggs and kippers in the air. Clova had been shown footage during a history lesson of an atom bomb being detonated. It felt as though another was about to go off. Inside her.

A girl walked by the door with her black, scruffy dog pulling on its leash.

This could wait. Clova knew exactly where she needed to be.

She slipped out the door and nudged her way through the crowds. The ground beneath her feet changed from carpet to flagstone and finally soft grass. The breeze was warm on her skin. She smelled the coconut perfume of yellow gorse flowers as she hared across the field. Clova cleared the burn in one leap and tore up the embankment, checking the road was clear at the top. She sprinted along the driveway and skidded around the corner.

She came to a halt outside the barn. Clova opened the door and stepped inside. The straw had been swept up. Tatty's water and food bowls had disappeared. His lead was missing. All that was sitting on the ground was the blue threadbare ball he loved.

Tatty had gone.

CHAPTER 11

Clova rested her head against the window of the car. Officially, she was grounded. Her dad had been furious with her when she'd got back from Stoneburn Farm. Clova hadn't listened to him banging on about her behaviour. She had been too upset that she'd never see Tatty again. That she had been robbed of the one thing that made her life bearable. Finally, when her dad had stormed off into the bar, she'd climbed the stairs to her room as though they were steeper than the slopes of Ben Attrin. Grandpa had brought up her dinner on a tray, but she couldn't touch it. He'd closed the curtains so she could no longer stare at the outline of the mountain that was as jagged as the serrated edge of a knife in the moonlight.

Clova had spent the next three days in her room. She couldn't even face going outside, not that her dad would have let her anyway. On the fourth day, Miss Willow had arrived all cheery with an iPad from school. She pushed her glasses up her nose and waved her hands around as though conducting an orchestra. Her over-abundance of enthusiasm was wearing. When Miss Willow spoke, all Clova heard was the blackbirds outside the window. Her attention shifted to the mountain. She fancied she could see deer crossing the rocky slopes in single file and was certain there were figures waving at her from the top. Her mind would drift off and she'd think about Tatty. She missed the tickle of his coat on her arms. His sweet straw and warm buttery popcorn-like smell. How he loved being chased when he had the ball. His eyes – big pools of amber that seemed to frame his thoughts. There were faint flecks of bright green in the corners of them, something Clova was certain nobody had ever noticed before. The realization that he'd gone for good would give her such a jolt, she'd find herself back in the room with Miss Willow, who'd still be droning on.

Grandpa switched off the car radio. "The Search and Rescue fundraiser total came in this morning." He changed down a gear to negotiate the hairpin bend. "Guess how much?"

She lifted her head away from the window. "Um. Two thousand pounds?"

"*Five* thousand pounds."

"That's the best so far," she said. "What will Search and Rescue do with the money?"

"They'll all go off on a cruise to Florida, I expect."

Clova rolled her eyes at him. That was the last thing the team would do.

He chuckled. "They'll be looking for some more equipment. Isla's raised the issue of Rannoch nearing the end of his working days. They'll need to think about training another dog soon."

Clova slid down in her seat. She shoved her hands in her pockets and turned her head away, embarrassed at how upset she felt.

"He's not retiring yet, Clova! It's right for Isla to bring this up now as it takes time and money to train a dog. And Rannoch has earned himself a life of leisure. He deserves to keep dry and stay by the fire when there's a howling gale outside."

"What if he's bored?"

"Then he could keep on working as a therapet."

"What's that?"

"A dog that goes into hospitals or care homes to comfort people. Research has shown that when someone interacts with a dog it slows their heartbeat down and lowers their blood pressure. They cheer people up. Dogs are good for us."

Clova thought of when Tatty had run around the barn, his hair sticking out all over the place, making his ball squeak. He'd really made her laugh. She missed the collie so much. Going outside was a chore without having his company to look forward to.

Grandpa pulled the car into a parking space on the main street in Glenstrome. He went into his wallet and brought out a fiver. "Go and get yourself an ice cream."

"Thought I was supposed to be giving you a hand with the shopping?"

Grandpa studied her face. The light that had been in her eyes seemed to have dulled ever since the Search and Rescue fundraiser. Lately, she appeared around the hotel like a ghostly apparition. Sometimes her presence was so fleeting, he wondered if she'd been a figment of his imagination. "I know it was the first fundraiser without your mum being there. Your dad and I found it hard going. You must have too."

She took the money and got out of the car. A bus passed by them.

"You're not going to get on it and head for the bright lights of Edinburgh to seek fame and fortune, are you?" asked Grandpa.

"Not with five pounds to my name."

Grandpa laughed. "I'll meet you back here in half an hour then."

Clova walked along the street, avoiding the cracked paving stones. She stopped outside Snow and Rock, which sold outdoor gear for walkers and climbers. Her mum had joined forces with the people in the shop to do guided walks up Ben Attrin for the tourists. Because they'd become friends, her mum would always stick her head around the door to say "hello" if she was in town. The lady who ran the shop, Lisa, waved at Clova. She waved back and then scooted away before Lisa could pop out to speak to her. She wasn't in the mood to pretend everything was OK.

Clova made her way along to Olive's Ice Cream Parlour. Inside, she leant against the counter as she decided what to have. She'd usually choose two scoops of raspberry ripple with extra raspberry sauce. Today she wanted something different. She pointed to the Mint Choc Chip. Clova and Sally would come here all the time after school. Even in the winter because the hot chocolate was every bit as good as the ice cream. She glanced around. The table at the back was where they would sit. On the wall hung a picture of two small figures skiing down a large scoop of ice cream that looked like a snow-covered slope. *That'll be us one day,* Sally had said.

Some of the ice cream dripped on to her hand. She left the shop and stood outside wondering which direction to go in. A girl came into view at the end of the road.

It was Sally!

For a moment, Clova wished she could tell her all about Tatty and that now he had gone, she had no one to talk to. And that her dad was barely speaking to her, and he'd managed to ruin what was left of the holidays by arranging for Miss Willow to give her extra tuition. She wanted to say that going up to First Year at the new school would be terrifying without Sally. And most of all, she missed how they'd laugh so much their bellies would ache.

Clova couldn't deal with being blanked by Sally again. She ducked down a dingy alley-way crammed with overflowing bins and sped along the uneven cobblestones. At the end of it, across the road, was the entrance to the park. She hurried over to it and glanced behind her, greatly relieved Sally was nowhere in sight. Clova strolled around some circular flower beds. She wasn't sure what the plants were, but they were red-and-white and striped like sweets. Trees and shrubs grew all around in perfect, manicured shapes. There was an oval pond in the centre of the park: home to a couple of swans, several ducks and some noisy coots. It was like being in a completely different world compared to the Drovers. Her mum had once told her that plants, flowers and trees were always locked in a fierce battle for space, light and water. Hard to imagine they were at war when this place was so sculpted and pristine.

Clova put what was left of her ice cream in the bin and sat on one of the benches. A mother and daughter strolled past – the girl chattering away as her mum smiled. Clova drew her coat around her. She had never felt so alone.

On the other side of the pond, a dog trotted to the edge of the water for a drink. It was a collie and had a scruffy black coat that looked as though it had never been brushed. There was a white stripe down the front of its face. The dog's tail was up in the air as he sniffed the ground and then trailed a scent across the grass.

Clova shielded her eyes from the sun trying to get a better look. Her heart fluttered as if there were Painted Ladies, Meadow Browns and Speckled Woods trapped inside her chest.

She leapt up. She'd recognize that coat anywhere! And those tufty ears that would look crimped in the rain! Clova resisted the urge to shout his name in case she startled him. She sprinted along the path and rounded a bed of gaudy flowers. Tatty sniffed at the leg of a bench and then bounded into the bushes.

Typical, she thought. *He'll be on to something interesting like the scent of a fox.*

Clova needed to see Tatty more than anything right now. He could put a smile on her face. He made everything better.

She crashed into the bushes, pushing leaves out of the way, her feet sinking into mud as soft as cake mixture. The branches slowed her down as she slid around. When she reached the other side and stepped out on to the path, she couldn't spy the collie anywhere. To her left was a wooded area and to her right was a large expanse of grass, which she hurried over to. There were lots of dogs in the park today, but none on this side were Tatty.

She turned on her heel and headed for the trees where she wandered around, hoping to catch sight of Tatty. At last she heard a dog woof – and a boy laughing. That must be Tatty! Clova couldn't wait to scratch the bit on his neck that made his ears slide forward and his eyes half close. To smell his warm buttery popcorn and sweet straw scent. To gaze in those amber eyes that were so beautiful they made time stop. Nearing a small clearing, she spotted a child and Tatty up ahead. As she came closer, the collie dropped his ball and barked at her. The little boy got a fright and burst into tears.

His father appeared and the boy ran towards him. He picked his child up and stared at Clova.

"I'm so sorry. I think I gave your boy a fright. It's just that I know this dog."

The man hitched his child further up his hip. "You know Rocky?"

She glanced at the collie, who was sniffing the air to catch her scent. That's when she noticed the dog's eyes were bright blue.

It wasn't Tatty!

"My mistake. I thought it was… I'm afraid I got it wrong." She backed away, not able to explain herself.

Feeling the loss of Tatty all over again, she stumbled through the trees. She checked her phone. She was late. Grandpa would be waiting for her back at the car. Clova spun around not knowing which way to go. She couldn't believe she'd thought that was Tatty. She'd been so stupid. Of course, she'd never see him again. He'd gone to start a new life with a new family. By the time she found the path again, her cheeks glistened with tears. She didn't even notice the man making a beeline for her until she heard the familiar voice of her grandpa.

"I thought I might find you here and not in the shops. It's exactly where your mum would have headed."

She hugged him, not wanting to let go.

"Och, lass. It's hard, isn't it? Especially when everywhere you go a fresh memory pops up you had forgotten about. And even though you can see them clear as day as if they're right in front of you – you know they're not coming back."

Clova wiped her eyes. She let her grandpa steer her out of the park. She felt so tired she wasn't sure she had the energy to make it back to the car.

"I bet you I can guess what flavour of ice cream you had," he said.

Clova was grateful he had changed the subject. She cleared her throat and sniffed. "What did I have then?"

"Mint Choc Chip," he replied with confidence as they crossed the road.

She hesitated, wondering how he could have possibly known that.

"I'm not just wise. I have psychic abilities, don't you know."

Clova frowned. "Did you see me in the shop?"

"You have Mint Choc Chip on your top," he said.

Clova glanced down at a line of bright green splodges.

"Come on, let's get you home, mucky pup. I believe there's a cup of tea waiting with your name on it. And some Vanish. That should take care of the ice cream. It'll be as good as new once I'm finished with it."

Clova rolled her eyes. "You don't even know where the washing machine is."

"You can draw a map for me when we get back," he said.

Clova was so glad Grandpa was here. He always had a way of making everything better.

CHAPTER 12

"Why are you called 'Clover'?" Kallum stood on the rocks. He found a stick and started hitting the water with it, breaking the trees reflected on its surface.

"It's not Clove-*er.* It's Clo-*vaaa.*"

The boy snapped the stick in half and threw it into the river. "What kind of a name is that?"

"I'm named after Glen Clova." She didn't mention that her mum had called her this because she had worked there one summer, fallen in love with the place, and, according to her dad, had then fallen for him. That part of the story had always made her mum snort.

Kallum's younger brother, Alby, crawled towards Clova. He held a stone and grinned as though he was holding a priceless artefact. He jabbed at it with a pudgy finger, liking the feel of the green moss covering it. Clova gave him a big smile and clapped her hands. Alby squealed with delight and toddled off to excavate some other treasure from the riverbank. Whenever he neared the water or nettles, Clova leapt up and steered him to safety.

Kallum took his red hat off and swiped it through the air at a cloud of midges above his head. "Dad said you lost your mum on the mountain. Could you not find her again?"

Clova was taken by surprise by his question. She pretended not to hear him and clapped as Alby brought her a leaf. She took it from him and he giggled.

"I would never lose my mum. That's stupid." He clenched his teeth together and gave a roar. Alby turned to see what was going on and pointed at his older brother.

Clova's grandpa had suggested that she could mind the boys while their parents, who were guests at the hotel, went white-water rafting. And, if she managed not to lose them, she'd be rewarded handsomely. At this point in time, she wasn't sure any amount of money would compensate for being with Kallum. Alby was no trouble at all. He delighted in everything around him until he grew hungry or was shoved to the ground by Kallum, and then he cried so hard rivers of snot ran down his face. But despite Kallum being a pain, it was better than being stuck in the hotel – or even worse, in the dining room with Miss Willow.

It's not that Clova disliked her teacher, it's just that her brain refused to concentrate when it came to the lessons. Miss Willow's smile never faltered. And she never raised her voice if she had to explain something for the umpteenth time. She'd not even batted an eyelid when Clova released a longhorn beetle on to the table. There was nothing Clova could do or say to make Miss Willow throw her hands in the air and leave for good. Miss Willow got under Clova's skin. She was cheery. All of the time. Clova began to wonder if her teacher actually had an *off* button. After every lesson, Miss Willow reported back to her dad. One time, Clova had walked into the bar to find them laughing. Miss Willow had thrown her head back as though it was the funniest thing she'd heard in the world and she'd touched Dad's arm – the way her mum used to. That had annoyed her the most.

Tatty was in Clova's thoughts all of the time. Was the fire in his amber eyes burning brighter at home with his new family? Had he forgotten her already? Sometimes a gloom would drift in like the mist over the moors, and Clova felt numb to everything as though she'd been wrapped in layer upon layer of spider's silk. There were days she'd look out the window and barely even notice the mountain.

At least with Kallum and Alby she couldn't dwell too long on the thoughts that spun around inside her head.

"Right, you two. Time to go," she said to the boys.

"We don't need looking after, Clov-*aaaghh*." Kallum balanced himself on the very edge of the rock and then wobbled. The water beneath him wasn't deep and there were stones everywhere.

"Come down from there!" she yelled.

He stayed put and pulled a face.

Clova eyeballed him. "There are two reasons why you should be glad I'm looking after you: one is I know where to find juice, crisps *and* cartoons; and the other is goblins live here and they don't like naughty children."

Alby screeched as he toddled as fast as he could towards Clova. When she caught him, he showed her his gums. Kallum hesitated before he clambered down from the rock and stamped through the shallows of the river. His hat fell off into the water. Clova raced after it, caught it and wrung it out. She handed it back to him.

"What do goblins look like?" asked Kallum, holding the hat away from him.

"They're green with pointy ears, sharp teeth and hooked noses. The biggest giveaway is their eyes, which glow in the dark."

"You're talking poop."

"Goblins also eat boys who are rude."

"Where do they live then?" Kallum scratched at a scab on his elbow.

"They can be found near rivers and on the moors."

"I'm thirsty. I want fizzy juice," said Kallum, changing the subject.

"Follow me." Clova took Alby's hand and steered

him up the embankment. Kallum scrambled up behind them, careful to avoid the rabbit holes.

After giving the boys juice and letting them watch some cartoons, their parents arrived back at the hotel full of tall tales about giant rapids and waterfalls. Kallum had asked them if they'd seen any goblins, which made them laugh. After they'd thanked Clova for looking after them, she made a swift exit and headed to her room. She tried to listen to some music. And then picked up a book, but after reading the same line four times, she put it back on the shelf. She felt under her pillow for the collar she had bought Tatty.

There was a knock at the door and Clova shoved the collar into her pocket. Grandpa stuck his head around the door.

"I think our egg fairy must be on strike. One minute we are overrun with them and the next we have none. I'm going to need some for the breakfasts tomorrow. Could you go over to Stoneburn Farm?"

She pulled a face. "Do you really need me to?"

"I wouldn't ask otherwise."

"Could you not go to the supermarket?"

"I've got guests checking in and I need to talk to the Tullochs about the hike they're going on tomorrow."

"I'm still grounded."

"I hereby, officially, unground you and grant you freedom in a one kilometre radius around the hotel, excluding the moors." He waved his hands in the air as though casting a spell.

"We could ask Isla to bring some?"

"Anyone would think you'd rather be surrounded by these four walls than experience the abundance of fresh air and natural beauty right outside your door."

Clova eyed him. He could read her like a book. She was reluctant to go. She didn't relish the thought of going back to the farm.

"All right, I'll go."

"Wonderful. Thank you." Her grandpa left her in peace.

Clova put a hoodie on and grabbed her rucksack. Outside, the clouds were so low they chopped the top of Ben Attrin clean off. She stomped through the field, aware of the air cooling around her. Mum would say it was often a sign that rain was on the way. She also said that if a pine cone was open, it meant the weather would be good. But she dismissed the old wives' tale about cows lying down before it rained as nonsense. They were resting. Raising calves and providing milk was exhausting work, after all.

Clova thought about Tatty. One time, when they were in the field, his ears had gone up and he'd frozen on the spot. Without warning he'd pounced and Clova had heard a faint squeak. The collie had been hunting tiny voles that lived in the grass. Luckily, the vole lived to tell the tale. As the memory faded, so did her smile. She stormed off towards the burn, jumped over it and hurried up the pitted drive. Something she'd done so many times before. Except this time her heart wasn't as light because Tatty wasn't here.

Clova halted and bent to catch her breath. Sometimes everything slammed into her like a wrecking ball: her mum. Dad. Tatty. Sally. Hating school. Having to put up with Miss Willow. Sometimes she felt as though she was teetering on the edge of a cliff.

She couldn't quite face Mrs Cairncross yet. It would be too hard to hear how Tatty was doing in his *perfect* home with his *perfect* family. Clova slipped past the farmhouse and made her way to the barn where she could sit for a while. She opened the door and closed it softly behind her. The sparrows fluttered around the beams above her head and the walls creaked. The place was warm and smelled of wood, dust and metal. Rain began to tap lightly on the roof. Clova took a crate down from the pile and sat on it. She remembered the day Tatty had trotted off with his ball, making it squeak. And him snaffling up the chicken when she wasn't looking.

All of a sudden the barn door flew open. Mrs Cairncross glanced around and then spotted her. "What on earth are you doing in here?"

"Coming to see you about some eggs."

Mrs Cairncross brushed the rain off herself. She perched on a wooden workbench. "This place was built in 1954 by my father. It's survived seven storms, twelve barn dances and a rampaging bull. I like it here too. It can be like sitting in a church at times. There's a peacefulness that allows you to gather your thoughts. As lovely as it is, I think you're here because you miss a certain four-legged friend. Would I be right?"

Clova nodded. Curiosity finally got the better of her. "How is Tatty?"

"Oh, he's on fine form."

"Has he settled into his new home?"

"Took a while to come out of his shell. For the first week, he stayed behind the sofa. But with some encouragement and treats he began to come out. What he wasn't so keen on was the hoover and the washing machine. And what he was terrified of was the children screaming."

Clova's face fell. "Is he OK?"

"Last time I saw him he was a little downcast, but he perked up."

Clova hated to think of him unhappy.

"Come on. Although they missed you, the hens have been hard at work. I've been making more cakes than the *Great British Bake Off*." Mrs Cairncross led the way into the courtyard. "Could you do me a favour while I collect the eggs? I've left a blanket in the paddock. Could you fetch it for me?"

"Of course."

The rain had stopped. The air smelled of damp earth and wet leaves. Clova strolled past the farmhouse on her way to the paddock. She wasn't at all pleased Tatty was finding it hard to settle into his new home. She realized Tatty being happy meant the world to her.

She swung the gate open and walked into the field, scanning it for the blanket. Out of the corner of her eye, something moved. It came barrelling towards her with tufts of fur sticking out all over the place.

"Tatty!" Clova dropped to her knees. The dog came tearing over, half yelping and half barking. When she opened her arms, Tatty tucked himself in close and nuzzled her cheek, his breath hot on her face. His amber eyes were the most beautiful she'd seen. Full of curiosity, wildness and wisdom. How she'd missed them! Clova buried her nose in his fur. The first thing she smelled was a strange perfume – and then the familiar scent of sweet straw, earth and warm buttery popcorn. His tail never stopped wagging. Her eyes filled up. She'd longed for this since the day he'd left.

"Surprise!" Mrs Cairncross leant against the gate and laughed. She'd never seen Tatty like this before. Nor Clova. She hadn't realized how close the pair had grown. "That dog has some nose. He knew you were here. That's when he perked up."

"Mrs Cairncross? Tell me he's here to stay?"

"The family are upset they can't keep him. They worked with a dog trainer and they made good progress, but he just wouldn't settle. It wasn't his fault. I've to let the rehoming centre know he's back. In the meantime, he's welcome to stay."

It wasn't quite the news Clova hoped to hear, but at least he'd be at the farm for a while longer.

"We may as well get him settled for the night," said Mrs Cairncross.

Clova clipped Tatty's lead on. As soon as she did, she was dragged out of the field at high speed. But she didn't mind at all.

Sniffing the ground, Tatty headed straight for the barn.

"Should I put some straw down?" asked Clova.

"Wait a minute." Mrs Cairncross left and returned minutes later with a fancy dog's bed. "They wanted him to keep it." Tatty also had new feeding bowls, a woollen blanket and a pheasant squeaky toy. Clova reached into her pocket and brought out the red tartan dog collar. She took his old one off and clipped the new one on around his neck. Tatty shook himself; the silver bone jangled.

"Very stylish," said Mrs Cairncross. "He's quite the dog about town."

Clova picked up the heavy chain attached to the pillar. "Tatty knows us. He doesn't need this, does he?"

"Let's keep it off him tonight. See how he goes."

Clova stroked Tatty's back. He half closed his eyes and settled into his bed. She didn't want to leave him, not after finding him again, but she had to go home.

Mrs Cairncross walked Clova into the courtyard and handed her a bag full of eggs.

"Will we be seeing you tomorrow, Clova?"

The sky had darkened and a breeze stirred. This time the rain began to fall in earnest. Clova pulled up her hood. She didn't mind the downpour. Not when she had her Tatty back again.

"Just you try stopping me, Mrs Cairncross."

CHAPTER 13

Clova looked up at the mountain. The damp clung to the grass and plants around them.

Her dad had gone off fishing for the day and Grandpa was busy at the hotel. It was one of the few times Clova could slip out on to the moors. She had missed their ruggedness and wild beauty. The paths her mum had shown her were etched in her mind. Each twist and turn yielding a new memory. There was a stillness about the place that made conjuring up her mum's voice easier here than it was in the hotel. She remembered her mum telling her mountain hares changed their coats in winter from brown to white. Clova had made her mum laugh by asking where they kept their wardrobes. For a fleeting moment, she could almost sense her mum walking beside her.

Clova called Tatty's name and he trotted back towards her, ears up, wondering what was going on. The family he'd stayed with had worked on his recall and all the other basic commands too. His actions were slick. There was an understanding in his eyes of what was wanted of him. Clova rewarded Tatty and brought out the long-line from her rucksack, swapping it for his shorter lead. Her stomach was in knots. Clova knew from all the times she'd watched Isla training Rannoch that at some point she was going to have to drop the leash and trust that Tatty wouldn't bolt. But if he did, he'd be easier to catch with the long-line trailing behind him.

Tatty trusted her.

She had to trust him.

It was now or never.

Clova let go of the end of the leash. Tatty zipped off at speed. Clova lost her nerve, put her foot down on it and picked it up. If he chose to run towards the mountain, he might never be seen again. The place was vast and Search and Rescue didn't do call-outs for missing dogs.

She held her breath. Doubt clouded her mind. She had to do this. She had to give it another go. She dropped the end of the long-line. The leash cut through a burn, became coated in mud and then disappeared amongst the heather.

Clova tried her hardest not to panic. "Tatty, come! *Tatty!*"

She heard a noise and the collie bounded back to her, the long-line still in tow. She rewarded him with a treat. Tatty left again, splashing through another burn and then returning to the path where he shook himself. The leash caught on a stone. Clova freed it and let go of it again. This time she felt a little bit more confident.

Tatty kicked up his heels. Full of life, he followed scents, climbed on top of rocks, darted between the bracken. There was a purpose to his stride; he knew exactly where he wanted to go. Every now and again he'd retrace his steps to see where Clova was. It appeared they were both keen to keep an eye on each other.

Seeing him free filled her with happiness. She chased after him. Tatty flattened his ears and zoomed around her until she became so tangled up in the long-line that she couldn't move and fell over. As she sat laughing, Tatty came over with his ears raised as if he wanted in on the joke. He was soaking from wading through so many deep boggy burns and shook himself, spraying her in mud. She undid the tangle, picked up the long-line and took up the slack. Up ahead was a giant boulder that had a spindly tree growing from it. When she'd asked her mum who had put it there, she had answered that, thousands of years ago, Scotland had been covered in ice and when it melted, giant rocks plucked from mountains were left behind on the landscape. Tatty and Clova climbed up and sat on it. The moors stretched out before them in muted browns and greens. From here, the Drovers looked like a small rectangular white box.

Clova brought out a flask of hot chocolate and a sandwich. Tatty glued himself to her side as she ate, his ears flying up every time she took a bite. She fished out a small piece of cheddar cheese and put it down for him. He sniffed at it. Then bowed and jumped back before returning for a closer look.

"Go on. You might even like it."

Tatty put the morsel of cheese in his mouth, gave it a couple of chews and then spat it out. Summoning up his courage, he hoovered up the cheese again, this time chewing on it with his mouth open as though it was a tough piece of leather. As soon as he finished it, he stuck his nose next to hers, wanting another piece. Clova brought out a water bottle and poured some into a cup for Tatty. He sniffed it and then drank it thirstily. When she'd finished her hot chocolate, Clova leant back against the tree. Tatty lay by her side, his ears and nose twitching the whole time. He kept a watchful eye on the moors as though he was guarding them. She put the water bottle and flask back in her rucksack. The cry of a buzzard made them both glance up. It circled around them and then glided away.

Clova caught sight of the mountain. Clouds had darkened and a mist appeared at the top of Ben Attrin. A breeze ruffled the back of her hair and Tatty's fur. It was time to leave. Even though the hotel wasn't that far away, if the mist rolled in, it would prevent her from recognizing the paths that were familiar and become impossible to navigate the way back home. Clova clambered down and let go of Tatty's leash. He scampered ahead on the path, out of view. She was determined not to stress out about the situation. There would be plenty of time to leave the moors. She checked behind to see tendrils of the mist now reaching all the way down to the foot of the mountain. It was moving fast.

When she turned back, Tatty had gone.

Clova felt the colour drain from her cheeks. Now was not the time to lose him. She stood, gripped with panic.

A memory of her mum popped up from nowhere. Her mum had kissed her cheek while struggling into her Search and Rescue jacket. *I promise I'll be back,* she'd said, as she hurried out the door. A hot coal had tumbled out from the fire on to the hearth.

She'd not seen her mum alive again.

Clova heard a noise. A deer that must have been resting clambered to its feet and bounded away in nimble leaps. She jogged along the narrow path, which was flanked on either side by peat hags and the tortured remains of Caledonian pines. It would be easy for Tatty to remain hidden if he wanted to. She raced back to the rock. Climbing on to it, she strained her eyes to see if she could see him.

As she whirled around on the spot in desperation, two grouse shot up into the air, as if they'd been startled. It had to be Tatty! Clova jumped down and took the path to the right. One second she was on the path, and the next she had to leap over burns and negotiate her way across boggy ditches. As she reached the spot the birds had risen from, she spied Tatty.

"Tatty!" she called, not able to keep the fear out of her voice. "*Tatty!*" He'd never come back to her if she shouted. She started to run, keeping him in her sights. To her great relief, Tatty slowed to a halt. He was sniffing at something.

When she caught up with him, he stood back, panting, his wet coat sticking flat to his sides.

Every hair on Clova's body rose. There was a red hat on the ground. He must have known it was here – just like the jumper she'd dropped in the field. She retrieved it from the puddle. It wasn't just any old red hat. It was Kallum's!

She looked up ahead. Had the family gone for a walk on the moors and he'd left it by accident?

Clova checked behind them. The mist had hidden the trees. She'd seen this happen time and time again. They'd have twenty minutes at best to get off the moors before they became impossible to navigate.

Tatty detected her unease and whined.

Clova began retracing their steps to the path she knew. Tatty refused to budge. She picked up his lead and gave it a gentle tug. Tatty dug his heels in. He faced in the direction of the river and wagged his tail, slowly.

What was the matter with him?

Clova returned to his side. Tatty didn't hesitate – he continued on down the path, his nose practically stuck to the ground. Once again, she tried to get Tatty to change direction, but he wasn't having any of it.

She brought out her phone to check if there was a signal. There were no bars on the screen. She stuffed it back in her pocket. What if Tatty was picking up on an old scent from earlier on in the day? And the family were all back in the Drovers while she was risking life and limb on the moors? Her dad would *kill* her if he knew where she was.

Tatty's ears pricked up. He bounded forward. Something or somebody must still be here. Otherwise the collie wouldn't be acting like this. She dropped the lead and ran after him until they reached a quagmire of mud. Working her way around the edges of it, Clova grasped on to handfuls of the heather in case she lost her footing.

Clova thought she could hear shouting. Or was it just the river crashing down from the mountain?

She crossed over some ditches. Tatty was further on ahead, barking.

They came to a small lochan, but there was no time to run around it. She stepped in and waded through it, the coldness of the water numbing her legs. She crawled out the other side and sped towards the river.

She couldn't believe the sight that met her eyes.

The river was churning over the rocks. A boy had fallen in and was being swept away. The water had carried him towards a pile of branches that had collected at the narrowest point of the river. He managed to reach out and grab on to the pile of wood.

The boy was screaming, which sounded thin and reedy compared to the boom of the river.

It was Kallum!

Alby stood further along, at the river's edge, crying. Clova shot towards him and pulled the child back to safety. She looked around wildly to see if there was something she could get Kallum to hold on to but there was nothing.

Tatty paced up and down, his tail between his legs.

Clova moved like lightning over to the collie. "Don't you run out on me, Tatty! You hear me?" She unhooked the dog from the long-line. He backed off, his ears flattened.

She waded into the river. The current was strong. She could feel the stones being sucked out from underneath her feet. If she lost her balance, she'd be swept away too.

She called over to Kallum to catch the end of the lead. She flung it to him but it landed short. She reeled it back in.

"Kallum. Take hold of the end."

Clova threw the lead out to him again, but Kallum didn't move. He was just a slip of a boy. The coldness of the water would be draining all his energy. She had to hurry!

Tatty began to woof. Alby had crawled forward again to the water's edge. Before she could yell Alby's name, Tatty barked at the toddler. Alby took fright and crawled away from the collie, crying. Tatty placed himself between Alby and the river.

"Your brother's safe, Kallum. We need to get you to safety too." Clova hurled the lead out. Kallum let go of the branches and grabbed on to it, the river swallowing him up. Clova cried out, dug her heels into the gravel, leant back and pulled with all her might. The lead went tight as it snagged on something in the river. Clova screamed in frustration. She could feel something give and the lead came free again. She gritted her teeth and roared as she tugged on the lead. As her muscles began to weaken and burn, she saw Kallum's head resurface. Clova dropped the lead and waded further into the water to lift him out.

She'd been on a Search and Rescue training exercise on the river and remembered what to do. Back on the bank, she laid him down, flipped him on to his front and slapped his back, until he coughed up all the water he'd swallowed. Clova sprinted to her rucksack where she fetched a jumper and her waterproof trousers. She changed Kallum into the dry clothes and gave him a biscuit. Clova then scooped Alby up and wrapped him in her coat to keep him warm. She had to get the pair of them back to the hotel as fast as possible. Clova checked her phone but there was still no signal.

"Kallum, do you think you can walk?"

He nodded his head and wobbled to his feet.

"Did you lose your mum and dad?"

His head hung low. "They wanted us to nap. But we weren't tired."

"Kallum, did you and Alby sneak out?"

"I wanted to find a goblin so it would know I wasn't afraid."

Clova's heart sank. She couldn't believe she was responsible for what had happened. "There's a bit of a walk to get home. I think a brave boy like you can manage, isn't that right?"

He nodded.

Clova couldn't put Tatty back on the lead because she would have to carry Alby. She'd have to trust he wouldn't run off. She watched as Tatty clambered up the riverbank and disappeared out of sight.

She picked up Alby and grabbed Kallum's cold

hand. As soon as they negotiated their way around the first lochan, she stopped dead.

"Clova? Why has everything disappeared?" whispered Kallum.

The mist had steamrolled in. Clova couldn't see more than a few metres in front of her. If the temperature dropped any further they'd be in danger of freezing.

Yet, they couldn't stay where they were because there was no shelter. Their clothes were soaked through and she didn't have a clue where she was. All she could hope was that Kallum and Alby's parents had noticed they were missing and alerted Grandpa. He'd call out Search and Rescue immediately.

But what if nobody was coming for them?

Tatty appeared out of the mist. He sniffed at the ground and trotted away from her again. But then he stopped and looked at her.

What was he doing?

Alby weighed a tonne and Kallum was exhausted, but she decided to follow the dog. He put his nose to the ground. She walked behind him. As they made their way around the edge of a lochan, she saw something white.

It was the paper bag her sandwich had been in. It must have fallen from her pocket. Then it dawned on her. The collie wasn't leading them on a wild goose chase. Tatty was using his nose to retrace their steps. It was something she'd seen Rannoch do, so why couldn't Tatty?

She got a tight hold of Alby and squeezed Kallum's hand as they walked on. The peat bog was relentless and slowed her and Kallum down. Alby had fallen quiet and she could hear Kallum's teeth chattering. She sped up and tripped, almost losing her footing. Everything her dad had said about the moors was true. It was just as dangerous as the mountain. An icy breeze whipped around them, looking for exposed skin to nip at. Clova was so cold and tired, she just wanted to lie down for a rest.

Somewhere up ahead, Tatty barked. It sounded strange in the mist. As if one minute it was close and the next kilometres away.

She stopped to hitch Alby further up her hip. Kallum clung to her legs.

Tatty ran towards them, barking.

Clova heard a shout. A thin shaft of light pierced through the grey.

"Kallum! Alby!" shouted a man's voice.

"Over here!" yelled Clova. She put Alby down and brought her phone out of her pocket to switch on the torch, making it easier for them to be spotted.

A figure loomed out of the mist. "Clova? Is that you?" asked Pete, squinting at them.

She stood blinking in the beam of his torch with her arms around Alby and Kallum.

"Bill! Over here!" Pete shouted. "You're safe now. I've got you."

CHAPTER 14

Clova finished the bowl of lentil soup. Now she knew why the Search and Rescue team loved it so much. It stuck to her ribs and warmed her from the inside out.

Kallum and Alby's parents had given them a hero's welcome when they returned. Except she hadn't felt like one. Not when everything had been her fault. In all the commotion, and the doctor arriving, Tatty had vanished and she had no idea where he was. Her grandpa had ushered her inside and insisted she change out of her wet clothes.

She couldn't bear the thought of Tatty being out in the mist all alone. And what if he strayed near Malachy Bain's sheep? He'd warned her he'd shoot the dog on the spot if he ever saw him on his land again. To add to her woes, Grandpa had called her dad. The cold on the moors would be nothing compared to her dad's iciness when he arrived home.

Grandpa sat a hot chocolate down on the table. "Drink up."

"Are Kallum and Alby OK?"

"Dr Cuthbertson declared them fit and healthy despite their ordeal."

Clova took a sip from her mug. The hot milk burned her top lip.

Her grandpa took a seat. "What happened this afternoon?"

"I found Kallum in the river and managed to get him out."

"You saved his life. He's an extremely fortunate boy, Clova."

She thought about Tatty. If it wasn't for him, she wouldn't have known the boys were there. It was the collie who had insisted they went to the river. For the first time, it dawned on her that Tatty was every bit as clever as Rannoch. Thinking back, when she'd had her hands full, he'd stepped in and barked at Alby to keep him away from the river's edge.

"What I can't fathom is why they'd sneak out on to the moors in the first place? I thought those two would be more into watching cartoons than having an adventure."

Clova pushed the cocoa away from her. She had to come clean about what had happened. "When I was looking after the boys, Kallum was being rude and acting recklessly, so I told him goblins lived in riverbanks and on the moors. It was to scare him off so he never went near them. Kallum left the hotel to go looking for goblins because he wanted to prove he was brave."

Grandpa gave a sigh and rubbed his eyes. "Clova, that wasn't your fault. I told your mother there was gold at the end of a rainbow, and guess what? She ended up in a field of cows with calves. She was lucky she didn't get trampled because cows can be protective of their young."

"How old was Mum?"

"Eight," he said.

"Same age as Kallum."

"You were trying to keep him safe. You had no idea what he was going to do. This story might have had a very different ending, but everyone is safe and that's what matters."

Clova sniffed and nodded.

They heard voices in the hallway. Her dad rushed into the kitchen. He flung his coat and fishing-tackle box down. "Come here," he said.

She stood, uncertain. Her dad pulled her towards him to give her a hug. "Clova, I'm so relieved that you and the boys are safe. What you went through must have been petrifying." He let her go and stepped back. "But what were you thinking putting yourself in so much danger, especially after everything I've said to you?"

She had been fooled by his hug. For a second she'd thought he cared. "Kallum had fallen in the river. I just wanted to get him out." She remembered seeing his body being pummelled by the water as it crashed into him. She shivered.

"Clova saved the boy's life, Jim. They're all back

here in one piece. Look at her, she's shattered. Maybe you can both talk tomorrow?"

Her dad pulled a face. "I'm trying to make her understand that she can't go taking risks out there. I don't care if she's tired. I'm tired. Tired of worrying about her – all of the time. What were you doing on the moors, Clova?"

There was an edge to his voice that made her uneasy. She wanted to tell him that she felt close to her mum on the moors. And that it was him who felt a million miles away from her. That the moors and the mountain were places she loved more than anywhere else. And she was more like herself there than in the hotel or at school. But she saw the anger in his eyes and nothing came out.

"Did you go because I've forbidden you? Is that it? And you want to disobey me – because I make your life such a misery? And so you want to make my life a misery too?"

"Jim…" Grandpa cast his gaze downwards and clasped his hands together.

Clova's dad carried on. "I'd barely left the place for five minutes. Can I not ever leave here again? Is that what you want?"

Sometimes her dad reminded Clova of the whisky he served in the bar: sour and sharp.

"Do you know what I think?" he leant in. "I think you want to follow in your mum's footsteps. You want to be the hero too. But we all know how that ended."

"*Jim!*" said Grandpa.

Clova ran from the kitchen. The walls of the hotel closed in on her. She couldn't breathe.

Two guests from Room 3 spied Clova and waited at the bottom of the stairs for her. "Here comes the hero of the day!" one of them said.

She gave them a tight smile and fled to the back door. She ran outside and headed for the fields. When she felt the grass under her feet she could breathe again. The cold woke her up like a slap to the face. She couldn't see the mountain through the mist, but she could sense it: dark and powerful and brooding. She staggered on until she could go no further and threw herself down under a tree. Everything was such a mess. She hadn't thought it possible things could keep on getting worse after her mum's death. It was like falling down a bottomless black hole. As she sat with her head in her hands, something nudged her. It was Tatty! His ears went flat and then he raised them.

She buried her face in his fur, his scent calming her. Her spiralling thoughts came back down to earth as the collie licked her face, his tail swishing backwards and forwards. And at that moment, it was just her and Tatty against the world. She put her arm around him and he leant in. "Nobody knows what either of us are capable of." He nuzzled at her pocket. "That's why you followed me, isn't it? Anything for a treat. Am I right? Or am I right?"

Tatty barked.

"Glad we got that sorted. Come on, let's get you back to the farm for some dinner and a rest."

She stood and brushed the grass off her jeans. Clova called Tatty. She didn't have to check to see if he'd follow. In the eerie quiet of the mist, they crossed the fields until Tatty charged past her. He bounded over the burn, and ran to the top of the embankment, where he waited. His coat wasn't as perfectly groomed as Rannoch's and he didn't hold himself the same proud way the Alsatian did, but Clova saw Tatty properly for the first time. Inside that scruffy exterior was an extraordinary dog with an impossibly big heart, who she never wanted to be parted from again.

*

Clova lay in bed, finally able to relax knowing that Tatty was safe and warm. There was a gentle knock at the door and her grandpa poked his head around it. "Can I come in for a minute?"

She sat up as Grandpa sat down. He passed her something. It was piece of paper that had been folded over. On it was a badly drawn stick girl. Inside the card it read: "Thank you. Kallum and Alby."

"Kallum wanted you have it. Something tells me he'll never be rude to you again. I had a quiet word with his parents about why they were out on the moors. They said he'd slipped out before at home, so they'll talk to him about it."

Clova put the card on the bedside table where it flopped over. She was relieved they were OK and that Kallum's parents weren't angry with her – unlike her dad.

"Do you mind if I ask a question?" said Grandpa.

Clova shrugged.

"It was fortunate you got to the boys when you did. What were you doing on the moors?"

She pursed her lips.

He held his hands up. "I come in peace. I'm not here to cause trouble."

Her voice trembled because she'd not said the words aloud before. "I feel close to Mum – out there."

Grandpa's eyes glistened. He sat in silence for a while. His granddaughter made him realize that he felt the same way. But not when he was in the wilds. It was when he was with Clova that he felt closer to her mum. Clova reminded him of her so much. He cleared his throat. "Isla called wanting to know how you were. I told her you were as feisty, stubborn, brave – and as insubordinate as ever."

"What does that mean?"

"Rebellious."

Clova snorted.

"When you rescued the boys, were you on your own?"

Clova frowned at him, puzzled.

"It's just Kallum mentioned something about a dog. Pete and Bill said they'd heard barking on the moors and that the noise of it had led them to you, but they hadn't seen anything."

Clova stared at her grandpa. She was bursting to tell someone about Tatty.

"Kallum was telling the truth."

"Was it Rannoch?" Her grandpa couldn't think of any other dog it might be.

"It was a collie called 'Tatty'. He lives nearby and I've been walking him." Clova put her pillow behind her. "When I first met Tatty, he was so scared he hid from me. I didn't think he'd ever show himself, but he did. I've been teaching him some of your basic commands – the ones from the notes you gave me. Grandpa, you should see him. He's such a fast learner. I thought he wouldn't be at all interested, but he's proved me wrong at every turn."

"That's why you were asking me about the dog training."

"It was Tatty who caught the scent of the boys. He found Kallum's hat. He knew they were still there!"

"Dogs can hear four times the distance of humans. It's likely he could have heard them."

"Tatty led me straight to the river. He's the reason

Kallum's alive. When I couldn't see a thing in the mist, he was retracing our steps on the moors before Pete and Bill found us." Clova's eyes were wide. "Grandpa, he would have led us all the way back to the Drovers, I'm certain of it." She shook her head. "I never saw it at first. I think he's got what it takes to be a Search and Rescue dog. Every bit as good as Rannoch."

The penny dropped. Grandpa realized the collie was the reason his granddaughter had a spring in her step of late. "Clova, training up a dog is hard. It takes hours upon hours of dedication. The pressure to help the injured or missing is huge. Lives are at stake. The dogs face desperately difficult and dangerous conditions – some that even us humans find impossible."

"But Rannoch manages. And he loves his work."

"He's an exceptional dog."

"I think Tatty could be too." Clova sat bolt upright. "Grandpa, come and meet him."

"Oh, Clova. I'm not sure."

"I'm not asking for any more than that. I just want to know if you can see what I do in him. That's all. Would you? Please, Grandpa?"

"What about your dad? You know how he feels about dogs at the best of times."

"It could be our secret, Grandpa," she said.

"There are no such things as secrets in Glenstrome. You know that. Your dad will find out sooner or later. Clova, if he discovers you were out on the moors with a dog then there's no telling what he'll say or do." He watched the last bit of hope disappear from Clova's eyes like dying embers in a fire. She slumped back against the pillow. Her mum's loss came back to crush her. He was surprised he didn't hear her bones crunch under the weight of it all. She pulled the covers up around her and turned on her side. The conversation was over.

He hated leaving her this way. "Tomorrow is a new day, lassie. Things will look better." He patted her foot and left the room, closing the door behind him.

Clova squeezed her eyes shut. In the dark, all she could see was Tatty.

CHAPTER 15

After the breakfast dishes had been cleared away and the rest of her chores had been completed, Clova ate some scrambled eggs for breakfast. Her dad had shut himself away in his room after their fight and hadn't appeared since. Marie was covering in the bar. Smells of furniture polish wafted along the corridors of the hotel.

Clova wanted to see Tatty, but she was feeling unsettled. She couldn't stop replaying what had happened with Kallum over and over in her mind. And then there was her grandpa. He hadn't told her to stop seeing Tatty, and yet he wasn't exactly encouraging about the collie either. It was the first time he hadn't been supportive and that made her feel let down and uncertain about what she was doing. She knew that if her dad found out she'd been on the moors with Tatty, she could be handing him the perfect excuse to sell up the hotel and move away. Yet, when she thought about Tatty, all the fear inside her melted away. It felt right being with him, no matter what the consequences.

Her grandpa walked in with a stack of dishes on a tray. "Isla and Rannoch are here."

Clova finished her eggs. She couldn't face Isla and Rannoch. Seeing them together, happy, was too much of a reminder she couldn't ever be with Tatty. "I've got work to do for Miss Willow," she mumbled. She stood, put her plate in the dishwasher, and brushed past him.

Grandpa watched her slope off. He cleared the plates into the dishwasher and then stood staring out the kitchen window for a while. Ben Attrin looked peaceful today: a mountain to be conquered rather than feared. Clova's mum had been so happy living here and working for Search and Rescue. He'd seen the same happiness recently in Clova, not realizing it had been because of a dog. He chuckled to himself that he'd actually thought it had been him who had cheered her up. She was so like her mum it was uncanny. A love of the outdoors. A quiet and determined strength about her. A natural ability to help others in times of need. A nurturing spirit. These were qualities to be admired and encouraged. Not punished. To see her so unhappy was torturous.

What kind of a message was Clova being sent, just because her mum had died on the mountain?

He grabbed Clova's red coat and marched up the stairs to her room.

She was sitting on the floor, scrolling through her phone.

He threw the coat over to her and she caught it. "Are we going somewhere?" she asked.

"Where's this collie you want me to see?"

"Stoneburn Farm," she said.

"Lead the way!"

Clova jumped to her feet, grinning. As they left the hotel, Clova waved to Isla. Rannoch bounded over and she felt bad she'd not wanted to see him earlier. The

Alsatian was always happy to see her. She scratched his back and he wiggled left and right when she hit the right spot.

"Enjoy your walk!" Isla shouted over. "And remember to leave some people for Rannoch and me to rescue, otherwise we'll be out of a job."

It was hard for Clova not to break into a sprint. She was so excited for Grandpa to meet Tatty. She marched through the field and chatted away as they crossed the burn and puffed their way up the embankment, where he pointed out a white-throated dipper, gathering moss for its nest.

When they reached the farm, Clova sent her grandpa to wait in the paddock for them. She opened the barn door and Tatty rushed towards her, wagging his tail. She made him sit and attached his lead. Then she kneeled to have a word with him. Tatty placed his paw on her leg as he listened.

"Now, Tatty. We need to show Grandpa how amazingly brilliant you are. Got that?"

Tatty's head tilted to the side. His ears went up and then dropped. He went straight to her pocket with the treats in it and sniffed.

The collie bombed out of the barn, pulling Clova behind him. She had to tug on the lead to steer him towards the paddock. Once he knew where they were going, he took off like a rocket from a launcher. As her grandpa watched on, Clova skidded through a giant puddle, nearly ending up on her backside. Tatty bounded into the field, dragging a red-faced Clova behind him.

Grandpa, who had been watching the spectacle, roared with laughter.

Clova shot him a look.

"Never seen an entrance like that before," he said, dabbing at his eyes.

"*Grandpaaa!* Don't stare! It's putting me and Tatty off."

Tatty shook himself and stuck close to Clova.

"Can I offer you some advice?" he said. "You are gripping on to the lead so tight, I can see the whites of your knuckles. You need to relax."

Clova looked down at her hands and loosened her grip.

"Drop the lead and shake yourself out."

Clova stared at her grandpa in disbelief.

"If you watch closely, you'll notice dogs shake themselves after a stressful situation because it releases tension from the body. Go on! Give it a go."

She glanced around to see if anyone was watching. Satisfied they were alone, she let go of the lead to shake her whole body. Tatty wagged his tail and woofed. She had to admit she felt a little less tense.

"The lead connects you to the dog. They feel everything through it: whether you're angry, sad, happy or tense. They can even detect adrenaline, so they know when you're scared and that can put them on high alert. It's important you're always aware of the message you're sending them."

Clova was astonished. She thought a lead was just that: a lead. She picked it up, remembering to stay relaxed.

"Tatty pulls on the leash, which tells me he's not used to walking on one. People think dogs automatically know what they're doing, but you need to show them. Walk around the paddock with him. Every time he pulls, change direction."

Clova began to walk and Tatty took off in another direction. She turned to take him the opposite way and when Tatty tugged on the lead again, she headed towards the gate.

"That's it, Clova. Keep the shoulders, arms and hands relaxed."

Little by little, Tatty stopped trying to drag her over to the tree or to the bushes. He began to walk with her so they were in step together.

"How's that?" asked Grandpa.

"Much better," she answered.

"Practise, Clova. He'll get the hang of it."

"Can I show you what else he can do?"

"Go on then." Grandpa took himself over to the wall, out of their way.

Clova dropped Tatty's leash. She took a deep breath and ran through the basic commands of "sit", "down" and "stay". Tatty listened and obeyed her, keen for a tasty treat. Until a pigeon landed next to them and then he tore off after it. Clova, remaining calm, called Tatty over. He ignored her and went for a piddle. Once he'd finished he charged over to her. She rewarded him with praise and a treat.

Grandpa took an object out of his pocket and threw it to her. Clova caught it. It was a thick piece of rope that had been tied at both ends. It looked exactly the same as the one that Isla had been using with Rannoch during the demonstration.

"Is this Rannoch's? He'll be upset if it is!" she said.

"Don't worry, it's mine. This is one of the first things Search and Rescue dogs learn – that work is play."

Clova raised her eyebrows at him.

"Let Tatty have fun with the rope."

Clova held the rope out to Tatty, who immediately took it between his teeth and shook it. She laughed and tugged back on it. Tatty let go of the rope by accident and then jumped around trying to get it back.

"Throw it to me."

Clova hurled it over to her grandpa who caught it. He waved it around in the air. Tatty galloped towards Grandpa and leapt up to grab it. Her grandpa then played tug-of-war with Tatty. When the collie released the rope, her grandpa threw it back to Clova. Tatty chased after it, keen to play some more.

"There, Clova. He's associating the rope with fun, so it'll become of high value to him. Once this happens, the next step is to hide it from him. So then he goes searching for it, because he really wants to play with it. If he was learning how to be a Search and Rescue dog, we'd use the same rope toy as the reward when he starts finding people in training exercises. And hey presto, he makes the connection between finding people and playing with his favourite toy."

"I can't believe saving lives is just a game to Rannoch."

"All that bravery for the reward of some fun. Isn't it incredible?"

"What about treats as a reward, Grandpa. Tatty loves them."

"Food is great to use in training. But the reality is when you're on a Search and Rescue mission it may be that you forget to grab the treats. The rope can always be part of your kit so it's more convenience than anything."

"Grandpa? Dogs get to play when they find someone. How about the Search and Rescue team members? Why do they do it?"

"Your mum once said to me she thought rescuing someone was like winning an Olympic medal. Only better."

"I felt terrified when I helped Kallum."

"You were put in a position where you were forced to be brave, without the proper training or experience."

"I know a bit."

"And that's why Kallum is still here to tell the tale."

Tatty flopped down on the grass, panting. Clova sat beside him. Tatty rolled over and showed her his belly. She rubbed it. "He's never done this before, Grandpa!" she said, her eyes shining.

"Dogs showing their bellies is a sign of trust and love."

Clova continued to scratch him. Tatty was in heaven.

She bit her lip. "What do you think? About Tatty?"

"I can see he's smart and keen to learn. He wants to please, which is good. But he's a work in progress, Clova. His attention wasn't always on you – he ran off after a pigeon. I know this might sound harsh, but can you imagine if that happened during a rescue? A life could be lost because there was a small furry animal the dog would rather chase."

Clova tried very hard to keep the disappointment from her face. She was convinced Tatty had something special, that, one day, he could be as good as Rannoch.

"It's tough being a Search and Rescue dog. They've got to work in the worst possible conditions; they're exposed to loud noises, all kinds of difficult terrain, other dogs, strange people who may be badly hurt. Does Tatty's owner know what you're doing?"

"He's a stray. Mrs Cairncross is holding on to him until there's a space for him at the dog rehoming centre."

"So he could go to a new family at any moment?"

"Unless…"

"There's more chance of you landing on the moon than your dad taking a dog in."

Clova sighed and plucked some grass off Tatty's coat.

"There was one thing I did notice."

Clova raised her head.

"I've trained hundreds of dogs and handlers. The best teams have a strong bond with each other. It doesn't always happen, but when it does you know that team will be a good one. You and Tatty have that bond, Clova."

"You hear that, Tatty? Grandpa thinks we are good together after all! That's something, isn't it?"

Tatty's tail wagged.

"Are you going to tell Dad about him?" Clova asked.

"I won't."

Clova breathed a sigh of relief. She tilted her head back enjoying the warmth of the sunshine on her face.

"But you will," he said.

Her head snapped back up. "*Why?*"

"Your dad needs to hear this from you and not anyone else. He has to know he can trust his own daughter. Nobody likes being lied to."

"He'll stop me from seeing Tatty."

"You don't know that for sure. But if someone else tells him – of course he'll do that. Give him a chance to prove you wrong."

Clova sat in silence. Her face set in stone.

"School will be starting back soon," said Grandpa, changing the subject.

She gave him the daggers. "Thanks for reminding me."

Tatty sat up and yawned in her face.

"If there's anything you need we can go to Fort William. We could even fit in a visit to the Grey Goose Café."

Her mum had loved the café because it was

perched on a mountain top. Clova liked it because you had to take a gondola to get there. She shrugged. "I do need new trousers and shoes."

"Your wish is my command. As long as they're appropriate for school and not something you'd wear to a disco."

"Nobody says the word *disco* any more. You go clubbing."

"Sounds positively Neanderthal."

"You're the dinosaur around here," she fired back.

Her grandpa burst out laughing. "I think it's time to go – you've managed to tire both Tatty and me out."

She put Tatty's lead on. On the way back to the barn, he pulled but it wasn't as bad as before. Clova settled Tatty in his bed, making sure the collie had some fresh water. She gave him a last treat before she said her goodbyes. Leaving him was something she found increasingly hard to do. She didn't linger and closed the door behind her.

Clova caught up with her grandpa, who was standing by the chicken coop. The hens clucked at him in a way that showed they were expecting food.

“So these are the famous chickens?”

“Grandpa meet Nancy, Sorrel, Betsy, Cluck and the one hiding in the corner is Mouse.”

His eyes twinkled. “I think I’ve just worked out who the egg fairy is.”

“I’ve no idea what you mean, Grandpa,” replied Clova as she walked on ahead of him, trying to keep a straight face.

CHAPTER 16

The school bus neared the hairpin bend and swung itself around it, taking up most of the narrow road. Clova let out a sigh of relief as soon as she saw the Drovers. She stood and made her way along the narrow aisle, trying not to bump into people. Finally, the bus slowed down and opened its doors. Clova was greeted by a blast of fresh air. It was as if the mountain wanted to wake her up after a day spent in stuffy classrooms. She felt like she'd been away from the place for a year.

As she began to cross the bridge, she was surprised

to see Grandpa. She sped up, concerned. "What are you doing here?"

He grinned and opened his arms out to give her a big hug. "I'm your official welcome home committee."

"*Grandpaaa!*" She stepped to the side. "People might see."

Behind her, the school bus pulled out from the stop. His hands flew up to his face in mock horror. "Oh, no! How dreadful that I missed you and wanted to make a fuss of you. Whatever will they think?" Not waiting for an answer he put his arm round her and squeezed her shoulder. "If you can't tolerate a show of affection, at least let me carry your rucksack."

She slipped it from her shoulder and handed it over.

"Well? How was your first day back?" They began to walk towards the hotel.

"OK," she replied.

"That good? Did you find the form room OK?"

"Uh-huh."

"Was your teacher nice?"

"Mr Keith? He seemed a bit grumpy."

"He must have been just as excited to be back as

you." Grandpa held the door open for her. "Did you win friends and influence people?"

Clova snorted. "It was my first day, Grandpa. Give me a break."

Her grandpa said his hellos to some guests and then whisked her off to the kitchen where there was a fresh pot of tea brewing and a flat chocolate cake sitting on a plate. Grandpa poured out two cups of tea and cut the cake into slices.

The kitchen smelled of warm sugar and washing-up liquid.

Clova lifted the plate up to examine it closer. "Did you make this?"

"With my own fair hands, but I forgot to add the baking powder and over whisked it. That's why it looks as though it's been sat on by an elephant."

"It tastes great, though." Clova wolfed it down, realizing she was starving. "Grandpa, did you like school?"

"I spent most of my time getting the belt or being in detention."

"Really? Can't imagine that."

"Let's just say I was not the upstanding, model

citizen you now see before you. School's not always easy, Clova. Well done for making it through the first day." He raised his mug of tea to her.

Clova was keen to change the subject. She cupped her mug, enjoying the warmth of it on her hands. "How's it been today?"

"Busy," he said with a knowing look.

"What have I missed?"

"The Glenstrome Police were here dealing with a report of hen harrier chicks being stolen from a nest. They wanted to rule out any possible suspects staying here."

"Oh no! Do you think that's possible?"

"We had one guest interested in the local bird life, but she was in her eighties. I think her days of shimmying up trees are long gone."

"She might have had an accomplice."

"I like your suspicious mind, Clova, however her companion was in his nineties. I imagine the sort of people who steal wildlife would be a bit more inconspicuous and stay in a van or a tent."

"I hope they catch whoever did it. Anything else happen?"

"Some folk musicians dropped in on their way to a festival at Fort William. After lunch, they brought out their instruments for an impromptu session. It was lovely to hear live music around the place – except now all the new guests think this happens every lunchtime." He raised his eyes to the ceiling and shook his head. "Isla and Rannoch came by for a chat. They'd been doing some training on the moors. Rannoch was looking everywhere for you. As they were leaving, he picked up on your scent across the car park to the bus stop. Isla had to call him back."

Clova would far rather have been here for all the comings and goings than being stuck in school. She wiped around her mouth and discovered a splodge of chocolate.

Grandpa cleared their cups and plates away. "What are you going to do now? Have you a monstrous heap of homework to do?"

"Not really – so I was thinking..."

"Of going to visit a small, scruffy, unruly creature who's in a barn not so very far away from here?"

Clova's eyes lit up. He could tell she was itching to see the collie.

"Can I? Please?"

Grandpa rolled up his sleeves and leant on the table, conspiratorially. "At risk of sounding like a stuck record about Tatty, you really need to think about telling your dad."

"Telling me what?" said her dad, who walked in the door with a tray full of rattling glasses. He placed it down by the sink.

Clova's face fell. "That I'd like to go out after being stuck in the classroom all day," she stammered.

"How did you get on?" he asked, loading the glasses into the dishwasher.

She shrugged. "OK."

"Did you see Sally?"

She dropped her gaze. "I did."

"I suppose going out for a short while wouldn't hurt," said her dad. He smiled as she leapt up and did a dance around the kitchen. Clova caught her grandpa's eye. He was frowning at her. She knew he wanted her to come clean to her dad about Tatty. But she wasn't ready to do it just yet. There was no way she would survive school without having Tatty to look forward to at the end of it.

*

Clova and Tatty crossed the field and slipped, unnoticed, into the woods opposite, where she put the collie on his long-line. Delighted they were together again, they ran through the trees, hopping over burns and squelching through mud.

"Oh, Tatty. I've had the worst day ever!"

Tatty jumped up on to a fallen tree that lay across their path. He tilted his head, listening to her.

"First of all I got lost. The school is huge and every single corridor looks exactly the same. I mean if there'd been a tree or a rock or a river there, I'd have found my way around no bother. So, I ended up being late and the whole class stared when I walked in the door."

The collie jumped down from the tree trunk, bounded up ahead and then raced back towards her. She held out her hand and he leapt up to touch her palm with his nose. "The teacher, Mr Keith, wasn't at all pleased. And you'll never guess who was sitting up the front."

Tatty trotted alongside her. "*Sally.* She stared at me as though she'd never seen me before in her life. I was so upset, Tatty. I always thought we'd go up to senior school together. Some of the other girls said 'hello', but nobody wants to hang out with me. Except for you, that is."

Tatty raced around her in circles, his lead making marks in the mud.

Clova stopped to examine some deer tracks. Somewhere, high up in the trees, she heard a couple of jays. Their calls sounded raspy, as if they needed hot lemon with honey for their throats. Three red squirrels leapt overhead and scratched their way further up the trunks. Everywhere she looked she could see a different shade of green. Clova found it soothing after a day spent in rooms with harsh, white, flickering strip lighting. Her stomach clenched at the thought she'd have to go back tomorrow.

"Mr Keith asked us to write about what we did over the summer holidays. I got into trouble, again. This time for not doing as I was told. What could I put in my essay, Tatty? That I struggled every single day because my mother's dead? Or that my dad thinks I'm an inconvenience who's not able to look after myself? Or that my friend and I fell out because I'm no fun any more? And I wasn't going to mention you because you're my business. Not theirs." Clova plonked herself on a tree stump, weighed down by her thoughts.

Tatty settled beside her. "No one was nasty or anything. There were loads of new faces today – people I'd never met before. But they looked at me in a way that felt like they knew all about me." She stroked his neck. "Maybe they think sadness is a contagious disease or something," she said more to herself than to the collie.

Tatty whined and nuzzled her cheek, making her smile. He tucked his head under her arm and pawed her leg. She ruffled his ears. "People make assumptions about you too, don't they? But I see the real you. And I think you're amazing."

Tatty gazed at her as though he was hanging on to her every word.

Clova glanced around the clearing. An idea came to her. She pulled out Tatty's ball. He'd been doing brilliantly at recall and finding his rope toy when she'd hidden it, but she wanted to try something new. "Here, Tatty!"

He bounded over. Tatty's ears shot up and he wagged his tail. Clova threw it as hard as she could into the trees. When she gave the command, Tatty took off after it like lightning. The second he was out of sight, she crept off into the trees opposite. She stepped on to a rock to cross a small burn and, as quiet as possible, climbed up a trunk and sat on a branch. She watched Tatty bounding back to the spot where they'd been standing only minutes ago. When he couldn't see her, he dropped the ball. Tatty sniffed at the ground. His nose sounded like a chuffing steam train as he followed her scent back to the tree stump where she'd sat. He stopped and looked around. There was a quickness to his movements; he was anxious he couldn't see her. Tatty whined and retraced his steps back to his ball.

Clova wondered whether she was asking too much of him. Just as she was going to call his name, he stuck his nose to the ground, entered the trees and headed towards her. Tatty followed her scent all the way to the burn, where he stopped. He paced up and down the water's edge, but lost the smell. When Clova was certain he was stumped, he splashed into the middle of the burn to smell the rock she had used as a stepping stone. He leapt over to the other side and sniffed all the way to the bottom of the tree she was in. Clova was so excited, she clapped her hand over her mouth to stop herself from making a noise. Tatty worked all the way around the trunk of the tree. He widened his search and then came back to the same tree. A squirrel leapt between the branches, making some leaves fall. Tatty glanced up and barked as soon as he spied Clova.

She clambered down and made a huge fuss over him. She wished her grandpa could have seen him in action today. She brought out his rope toy. Tatty grabbed it and shook it hard. After they'd had a spirited game of tug-of-war, she put the toy away in her pocket.

"Go, play!" she said.

He wagged his tail so much it was a blur. As they carried on through the woods, the collie's nose was barely off the ground. The place would be full of the smells of badgers, foxes, deer, red squirrels, pine martens, mice and stoats. It must be like the equivalent of walking through the perfume section of a department store. The fact that he found Clova's scent amongst everything else in the woods was miraculous to her. Tatty charged on up ahead, investigating ditches and the denser parts of the woods she couldn't enter. He dug a shallow hole in soft earth, drank from a puddle of water, rolled in some leaves and waited for her to catch up with him. Her heart burst with pride. How much he'd changed since they'd first met. How far he'd come along in his training.

Clova broke into a run and weaved in and out of the pine trees. Tatty galloped alongside her, his tongue lolling out the side of his mouth. She didn't care who heard her whooping at the top of her lungs.

CHAPTER 17

Clova spent as much of her spare time as possible training with Tatty. She was extra careful when she was out with the collie, so they weren't seen by her dad or by someone who might say something to him. Clova loved spending time with Tatty. She didn't ever want that taken away from her.

The days turned into weeks. The trees around the hotel looked as though they were on fire and then dropped their leaves, scattering in whichever direction the cold wind blew. Clova's grandpa took great delight in telling all the guests that Scotland had two seasons: July and winter.

School dragged on. A couple of the girls had asked why she didn't hang out with Sally any more. The library became her sanctuary from prying eyes. Clova read every book on dogs and training she could lay her hands on. The librarian began to put books aside that she knew Clova would enjoy.

Her breath misted up her bedroom window as she sat looking out across the snowy landscape. Ben Attrin wore a white coat that shone in the sunshine and glowed mysteriously in the moonlight. But it had a darker side: the snow made the mountain even more treacherous. She recalled her mum leaving the hotel for the last time: her jacket bright red against the bluey snow. After the accident, Clova had found her mum's boot prints at the back of the hotel, heading towards the moors. The day they finally melted, she had been inconsolable.

Her grandpa had said her dad would get better, but as far as she could tell, he was getting worse. All he wanted to know was where she was at all times. Or if she was working hard at school. He didn't even mention her mum. It had become too painful a subject for him. When she was awake, he slept. And when she was asleep, he roamed around the hotel.

After her chores, Clova couldn't settle. She didn't want to read. Or listen to music. Or watch TV. And she definitely didn't want to do schoolwork. But she had a good idea who might stop her from moping around.

She put her coat on and laced up her boots. Clova found her hat and wrapped a scarf around her. Before she could slip out, her grandpa caught sight of her. "Off somewhere?" he shouted down the hallway.

"Three guesses."

He walked towards her, clutching a sink plunger. "Your dad is picking up some supplies in the village, but he won't be long. If you must go out, take your phone. And please don't stray far. There's a high chance Search and Rescue will be called out today. This weather always causes mayhem out there – and in here. You know how on edge your dad gets when there's snow."

Clova huffed air from her mouth.

He held his hands up. "OK. OK. Lecture over and done with. I'm off to deal with a blocked sink in Room 4. Is there no end to the glitz and glamour of my life?"

Clova smiled. She and her dad would be so lost without him. He was the sticking plaster trying to heal the wounds between her and her dad. Without thinking, she gave him a hug.

"Help! There's an imposter! Would someone please give back my real granddaughter!" Grandpa chuckled before he disappeared off.

Clova stepped out into a world that was barely recognizable, loving the sound of her footsteps crunching in the snow.

*

Tatty must have heard her approach. He barked loudly inside the barn and scratched at the wood in his eagerness to see her. When she opened the door, he practically jumped into her arms. Clova clipped his long lead on and they set off. Tatty ran and sniffed all around, astonished by the snow. As soon as they reached the field, he galloped across it at high-speed and then skidded to a halt to taste the snow. Small balls of ice formed above his feet like anklets. Tatty put his nose down to follow all the scents, but there were so many of them, he ended up like a dog possessed.

Clova bent to scoop up a snowball, which she

shaped with her hands and threw at him. He jumped into the air and caught it. He landed and smacked his lips together as it melted in his mouth.

She practised some recall with Tatty and then buried his rope toy under a big pile of snow. Tatty sniffed around the same spot for ages. Without hesitation, he dug down through the snow until he found his most prized possession. He charged over to her with the rope toy, wanting her to try and steal it off him. She pulled hard and Tatty let go of the rope. She went flying back and landed in the snow. Tatty galloped over. He peered down at her, his ears covering his eyes. His whole body wagged with his tail.

Clova got to her feet. She brushed the snow from her hands and headed over to the burn. Part of it was frozen over. Clova was fascinated by the swirl of white lines on the surface of the ice, reminding her of isobars on a weather map. Tatty raced up, curious. The minute he stepped on to the ice, he skidded and shot across it into the bank on the other side. A laugh escaped from Clova's mouth. Tatty skittered over to her, losing all control of his legs. Finally back on non-slippery ground, he stuck his head under her arm and stood staring out over the fields towards the mountain.

Clova followed his gaze. Seeing Ben Attrin all white reminded her it wouldn't be long until the anniversary of her mum's death. According to her dad, the accident had happened fast. It had been snowing heavily for a few days, so much so that it had compacted into ice. On the morning of the rescue it had snowed again, a fresh layer forming on the surface of the ice. When Search and Rescue were on the mountain, the top layer of snow began to slip and turned into an avalanche. Her mum had been lower down in Raven Gully when it had struck.

A crow called out as it flew towards the trees.

Clova breathed in deep and let her breath out. Grey clouds formed in the air and drifted off. Her lips and cheeks felt tight in the cold.

Tatty went in search of a stick. He came back and dropped it next to her. He then ran to fetch another and didn't stop until there was a small pile of them at her feet. The collie seemed to know when she was sad. She patted him and checked her phone. She'd been out for over an hour now. Grandpa was right. There was no point in winding her dad up.

Tatty began to sniff at everything as they walked up the drive. Clova had a feeling he was putting off going back to the barn. She wished he could be with her all of the time.

Rounding the corner, she spotted Mrs Cairncross feeding the chickens.

Tatty went bounding over to Mrs Cairncross, who made a fuss of him. When Mrs Cairncross looked at Clova, her expression was troubled.

"Is everything OK, Mrs Cairncross?"

"There's something I need to talk to you about."

Clova didn't move a muscle.

"I'm just back from town where I saw your dad."

The hairs on the back of Clova's neck stood up.

"I told him that I thought you'd done a brilliant job with Tatty. That you had worked so hard training with him every day. I said that rehoming Tatty didn't make sense when the pair of you had such a close bond and asked him to reconsider taking the dog in."

Clova's blood ran cold. "He knows about Tatty?" Her voice was little more than a whisper.

Mrs Cairncross nodded.

Clova's eyes widened. "Why did you say that to him? Tatty was my secret."

"Your grandpa knew. I just presumed your dad did too. I'm sorry. If I'd known, I'd never have betrayed your confidence."

Clova's dad was going to kill her. He'd never trust her again. She'd never be allowed out to see Tatty. This was all the excuse he needed to sell up and move away.

Mrs Cairncross let out a huge sigh. "Your dad was furious. He threatened to call the rehoming centre if I didn't."

"Mrs Cairncross? Did you?"

"They're on their way."

Clova gasped.

"I'm sorry, Clova. So sorry. I'm only glad you got the time together you did. Look at him now. Tatty's a different dog. Nobody can take that away from you."

Tatty glanced up at them, knowing he was being talked about. He wagged his tail slowly.

Mrs Cairncross's eyes teared up. "I'll give you some space to say goodbye. Don't become a stranger. You're always welcome at the farm."

Clova led Tatty to the barn in a daze. She couldn't believe this was it. After everything they'd been through together. Anything had felt possible with Tatty by her side.

The time had finally come for her to face the facts. Her dad would never allow her to keep him. Tatty deserved a fresh start with his own family. The more people for his big heart to love the better. A full tummy, a fire of his own to lay in front of and a cosy bed. He'd thrive on new places to explore. A happy life awaited him beyond her and Stoneburn Farm. He'd make some lucky person the best companion.

Clova didn't want to prolong the agony. She fished around for his rope toy in her rucksack. When she brought it out, Tatty bounced over to her, excited.

Clova crouched down and the collie gave her his paw. She stroked his neck and Tatty licked her cheek. He raised his ears, waiting for the fun to begin.

"I'll never forget you." Clova stood and threw the toy across to the other side of the barn. As Tatty ran to fetch it, she slipped out and closed the barn door behind her. Tatty scratched at the wood as soon as he realized she'd gone. His howls echoed all around the farmyard.

Clova stumbled through the fields, numb. As she reached the back of the hotel, Clova caught sight of her dad through the kitchen window. He was shouting at her grandpa. None of this was his fault! She flew through the back door and tore down the corridor. When she entered the kitchen, Clova had never seen such a cold look in her dad's eyes.

"I had an extremely enlightening chat with Mrs Cairncross. It appears you've been sneaking out, going goodness knows where with a stray dog! Right under my nose. Can you imagine how that made me look? Not having a clue what my own daughter was up to?" Her dad's hands were shaking. She'd really done it now. A sense of dread washed through her.

"Did you know about this?" Her dad turned on Grandpa.

"I did," he answered.

"How could you just stand by as she was putting herself in all kinds of danger, when you specifically knew it was against my wishes?"

Clova took a couple of steps forward. "Grandpa wanted to tell you."

"I'm not speaking to you, Clova," spat her dad.

Grandpa gripped the back of a chair with his hands. "I'm sorry, Jim. I should have talked to you about it."

"Those training cards on her wall. All the times she's disappeared off for *fresh air.* Tiptoeing behind my back. How can I ever trust the pair of you again with all this going on? You've treated me like a fool." Her dad's face fell. "When she found those boys by the river, was she with that dog?"

Grandpa blinked. His mouth fell open slightly.

"She was, wasn't she?" roared her dad. "Which means she must have been on the moors with it. It was the dog that led her to the boys, wasn't it? The dog took her to a river that could have killed her. Have the pair of you lost your senses, because I'm struggling to get my head around this?"

"We never meant to hurt you. Or for her to be in any danger. I just wanted to see her happy again." There was a flatness to Grandpa's voice.

Her dad's face darkened. "Pack your bags. You're no longer welcome here, Archie."

Grandpa looked as though his world had collapsed around him.

Clova tugged on her dad's sleeve. He pushed her

away. "Dad! He begged me to tell you about the dog. He wouldn't let up about it. It's not his fault. Please, Dad! Please? It's not fair."

"I'll tell you what's not fair. The pair of you lying through your teeth to me."

"I was never in any danger because of Tatty. I think he could be every bit as good as Rannoch."

"Utter nonsense. You are living in a fantasy world, Clova. And it's not helped by your grandfather encouraging you. Mrs Cairncross has assured me the dog will be collected by the rehoming centre today. Let this be an end to it."

"But, Dad!" Clova's face darkened. She couldn't bear it. She had lost her mum. And now she was losing both her grandpa and Tatty. "I wish it had been you on the mountain. Not Mum," she said as she grabbed her rucksack and fled outside. Clova put her head down and turned her back on the Drovers. She ran as fast as she could towards the moors.

CHAPTER 18

Long plumes of snow drifted off the summit of Ben Attrin, forming wispy white trails in the sky. Her mum once said to her that the only times she felt her heart beating in her chest was when she was on the mountain.

Mum would never have told Grandpa to leave. She'd never have stopped her from exploring the moors and mountain. Clova felt certain her mum would have allowed her to keep Tatty. She carried on, fuelled by anger.

Clova heard water all around her: the rush of the

river, the gurgle of the peat bogs and burns. The drips of the now-melting snow hitting the ground. The crack and hiss of trapped bubbles under the ice as she stepped on it.

She moved at a steady pace as she wound her way around the network of paths she knew like the back of her hand. Clova passed the giant boulder where her and Tatty had stopped for lunch. She remembered how they'd watched over the moors, together. Something they would never do again. Fresh anger surged through Clova's veins. She powered on.

Sometimes the going was easy and other times she plunged into snow drifts up to her knees. Every step brought her mum closer. Some grouse fled noiselessly away from her. A memory came back of when they'd once caught sight of an eagle that had flown so low they could make out the feathers on the underside of its wings.

Her mum used to say that when you were out in the wilds you became aware of every little thing around you – like a wolf. Clova had been taught that a snow-filled landscape was not a desolate place but a world full of life. Her mum had shown Clova the delicate prints of the hare, which made a leaf-like pattern on the surface of the snow. Clova could spot the footprints of a fox and the indents of its bushy tail behind it. If there were some tracks surrounded by nothing else except for pristine snow, there was a good chance you'd find the burrow of a vole.

Clova reached the birch trees at the base of the mountain, somewhere she hadn't been since her mum's accident. It was both familiar and new to her at the same time. She remembered her mum showing her the network of badger setts that extended far along the first row of trees. She had been fascinated by the smooth heaps of earth beside their homes. Her mum had said badgers could dig up to three hundred metres of tunnels.

She heard the call of a raven. The wind stirred and the trees whined and clacked off each other. Every now and again clumps of snow would fall on to the ground with a soft whump. She could sense the presence of the mountain. Almost as if it was daring her to step on to it.

Clova shivered. She'd left in such a hurry she'd forgotten her hat, scarf and gloves. She sped up in an attempt to warm herself. As the ground started to rise upwards, she heard a snap of twigs. To her right, deer bounded ahead. Their bodies were a rich chestnut brown against the snowy backdrop.

She stuck to the path that wound its way past a river which flashed over mossy boulders and into a series of tiered pools. As she neared the top, she stopped to catch her breath. She turned to look down through the woods. The moors stretched out beneath her, mist rising off them in the sunshine. The Drovers was impossible to see in the snowy landscape. She breathed a sigh of relief that she no longer felt watched by the hotel.

Clova knew that if she pressed on just a bit further, she'd reach one of her favourite places: somewhere she and her mum loved.

Concentrating hard, she climbed her way up a steep bank. Each of her movements were so precise it became a choreographed dance between her and the mountain.

Reaching the top, she stood. To the side of her was a waterfall made out of hundreds of long white icicles. She'd never seen it looking so beautiful. Her mum would have loved this. Every summer, they would both come here to bathe in the pool. She could almost hear their shrieks of delight echoing around the place as they had stood beneath the falling water and lounged around in the pool afterwards, tingling from head to toe.

"*You'll always leave this place feeling better than when you arrived,*" her mum had said.

The pool was frozen over. Clova found a pebble and threw it up in the air. When it hit the ice, it bounced across to the other side, making the same sound as if it had landed on a thick sheet of glass. It was pleasing to her ear. Clova chose a heavier stone and dropped it near the pool's edge. Thick chunks of ice shattered.

It pained her that she'd never be able to come here with her mum again.

Clova hunted around for another stone. She hurled it at the icicles. There was a tinkling as some of them snapped. Shards of ice rained down. She threw another one. And another one. The icicles smashed as they hit the hard surface of the pool. Clova did it again and again and again, until her arm ached.

The sun dipped. The tip of the mountain was bathed in a golden light and the rest of Ben Attrin was cast in a dark blue shadow. Clouds blew over the pinnacle as if someone was fast forwarding the sky. Sad the day was coming to a close, the wind whistled a mournful tune.

Clova returned to the top of the slope. It would be dark by the time she got back to the Drovers and she wasn't wearing the proper clothing to protect herself from the cold. She patted around inside her bag and found her phone, an apple and a Twix bar. At least that was something. She checked the signal on her phone. Nothing, as expected. She placed it back in her pocket and slung the rucksack over one shoulder. Her mum's words came back to her about what Clova should do if she was ever unsure she could make it back to the Drovers safely. They'd been drummed into her since she was little. Clova wasn't to attempt the journey, but should find somewhere safe to shelter instead.

Although the woods would provide some cover, it would be safer out of the wind. Every year, she'd witnessed people being brought down with hypothermia, which was caused when the body's temperature became too cold.

Her mum had known every nook and cranny of the mountain. She had pointed out all the places for Clova to go if she ever needed cover. She remembered that not far from the waterfall was a small cave that could protect her from the worst of the weather. She stepped on to the iced-up pool. Nearing the other side, there was a loud cracking noise and her foot plunged into the water. The cold shocked her system. Pain travelled up her leg and around her body. She pulled her foot out and jumped over to the embankment. Her boot squelched as she walked towards the solid wall of rock. Clova followed the rock face around the corner, until she reached the cave. The entrance to it was a steep, flat slab of stone she'd have to scramble up. She stepped out on to it and her foot slipped. Clova lost her balance and shot towards the edge where there was a drop. Her rucksack slipped off her arm and plunged towards the forest floor below. She tried to grip on to something, but the stone was covered in black ice. She shrieked as she lost her hold and her body dangled over the edge. Clova daren't look down. She gritted her teeth as she hauled herself back up on to the rock. Using the last of her energy, Clova crawled into the small cave, at last sheltered from the elements. Her hip and leg ached where she'd fallen. She couldn't believe she'd lost her rucksack!

The wind picked up and howled around Ben Attrin. The noise reminded her of Tatty as she'd left the barn. She wished he was here with her.

Exhausted, Clova rubbed her eyes, which ached from looking at the bright snow all day. Her head thumped and her body felt stiff and bruised. She tried her best to dry her foot. Her wet boot, sock and trousers stole the last of the warmth from her body.

Bit by bit, the light dimmed to dark blue and then inky black. The stars showed up like hundreds of fairy light strings in the sky. Right at that moment, it felt as though she was the only person in the universe. Clova's stomach growled with hunger.

Bits of ice crashed down past her, making her jump. The mountain cracked, whined and rumbled as though trying to rid itself of its coat of snow and ice. All Clova could smell was the cold.

She wanted to pace up and down to keep warm, but she was terrified she'd slip again in the dark. Never had she been so chilled to the bone as this. She slapped her cheeks, arms and thighs and then stuck her hands in her pockets.

Time passed. As soon as she closed her eyes, all

she could hear was Grandpa's voice telling her it was dangerous to fall asleep in low temperatures. And when she opened them, she swore she could see shapes moving in the darkness. Her blood flowed like meltwater through her veins.

Clova pulled out her phone. It lit up, a soft beam of light offering some comfort in the dark. She scrolled through her photos. The first one was of Grandpa, smiling as if he'd just said something funny. She stared hard at it. She couldn't imagine the hotel without him. The second picture was a selfie of her and Sally goofing around – in the days they used to goof around. The next was a photo of her with Mum and Dad. They were at Four Rock Pass near the summit of Ben Attrin where they used to climb when she was younger. They loved that place. In fact, she was pretty sure it was her mum's favourite spot on the whole mountain. All three of them were smiling at the camera. It was strange seeing her dad so happy. She clicked the phone off to conserve the battery.

Clova was sorry. Sorry she'd not fought more to keep Tatty. Sorry she'd not been honest with her dad and sorry that this had caused trouble between him and her grandpa. She was sorry she'd never see her mum again. And she was sorry for venturing so far away from home. Her dad would be sick with worry. All of them would be.

Clova heard a noise.

There it was again.

Her head snapped up.

Was something there?

A dark mass skittered towards her.

Clova pushed herself as far back in the cave as she could go. She covered her head with her arms, bracing herself.

Something nudged her leg and she heard a whine.

"Tatty?"

She stretched her hand out to feel wet fur. Clova pulled the collie towards her and buried her nose in his coat which smelled of earth, sweet straw and warm buttery popcorn. Tatty nuzzled her face and then tucked himself in beside her. She felt his warmth immediately. Clova had no idea how Tatty had managed to find her. He was supposed to be at the rehoming centre waiting for his forever home. With the collie back by her side, Clova was no longer scared. She held on to him and finally allowed herself to drift off.

Clova woke with a start.

Tatty was whining.

Her mouth was dry. Everything came flooding back to her. She checked her phone. It was ten forty p.m. Her dad would be beside himself by now.

Tatty was as still as a statue. His ears shot up. Something had caught his attention.

Clova sat up and winced, hardly able to move her leg.

Over the noises of the mountain, she thought she heard shouts.

Was it Search and Rescue?

Tatty skidded out on to the slippery ledge. Clova inched forward on her hands and knees, careful not to slide. She spotted a line of lights that had moved past the waterfall. The team must be heading further up the mountain!

It would be treacherous in these conditions.

She tried to shout, but her voice was too hoarse. Clova clapped her hands and waved her arms, but it was about as much use as a damp flare.

Clova was well hidden. She had to attract their attention!

She patted around for a stone. Finding one, she threw it. It clacked a couple of times off the rock face and then … nothing.

Before she could stop him, Tatty leapt down from the ledge and raced over to the waterfall where she heard a splash. Then it went silent.

Had something happened to him?

Clova peered into the dark. She had to find out if Tatty was OK – and try to attract the attention of Search and Rescue. Terrified of slipping, she moved at a snail's pace.

The searchers' lights began to fade.

She made it across the rock and on to solid ground. Clova tried to stand, but a shooting pain in her leg stopped her. She shouted for help. Somewhere, in the dark, she heard barking.

It was Tatty!

Clova hauled herself on to her feet. "Tatty!" she called.

Tatty's barking became louder. Clova limped towards the waterfall. At that moment the wind whipped round the side of the mountain and stopped her in her tracks. She struggled against it, not sure how much further she could go.

Clova lost her footing and fell. Her hand shot out and hit cold water. The pool she'd crossed earlier was no longer frozen.

A light flashed. Clova blinked hard, wondering if her eyes had tricked her. She fumbled in her pocket for her phone. Her fingers were so cold she dropped it. Cursing under her breath, she picked it up again and held it up, turning the torch light on.

She was sure she could hear noises like someone moving around right in front of her.

All of a sudden, Tatty raced out of the blackness. He bounded over, barking and wagging his tail, showering her with spray from the pool. Isla followed on shortly behind.

"Evening! I heard this one barking so came back to investigate. Just as well I did. Are you OK?" she asked.

Clova tried to smile but all she could manage was a grimace.

"I know you like an adventure more than most, but I'd wager you'd be ready to swap all this for a warm bed and a mug of something hot."

Clova nodded.

Isla fished around in her rucksack and brought out a hat, scarf, gloves and an energy bar for Clova, who devoured it ravenously. Isla then gave her a huge hug before she updated the team and the Drovers on the walkie-talkie.

Clova heard a cheer go up.

Isla rewarded Tatty with a rope toy. He took it between his teeth and wagged his tail. "This is one clever boy."

"I think he must have escaped from Stoneburn Farm before the rehoming centre was able to collect him. He found me in the cave that's around the corner."

"Good job sheltering out of the wind, Clova. Was the pool frozen when you crossed it?" asked Isla.

"Yes."

"I'm sorry, Clova. We guessed wrongly that you wouldn't have waded across it in this weather. Thank heavens for Tatty barking. He must have tracked your scent across the ice just before it disappeared."

"How come it melted? It's so cold."

"We're on the lowest part of Ben Attrin. It's practically tropical down here compared to the top.

Plus the waterfall is sheltered from the worst of the weather."

Clova shuddered, glad she wasn't higher up on the mountain. She couldn't possibly imagine being any colder than she already was. She glanced around. "Where's Rannoch?"

"Lounging in front of a roaring fire with a large cone around his neck. He cut his paw on the farm today. Needed stitches. He'll be out of action for a while, but he'll live to fight another day."

Isla hooked her arm under Clova's to support her.

"Is Dad going to kill me?"

"He'd better not after we've gone to all the bother of rescuing you!" She softened her voice. "Trust me, he'll be very relieved and grateful to see you, Clova. Come on! Homeward bound we go."

"I'm sorry, Isla. I should've known better."

"All that matters is that you're safe and well. Besides you couldn't have picked a better night for it, Clova. The stars are out in force; you can even see the Milky Way. Plus I'll be able to scrounge some of your grandpa's lentil soup. There are worse ways to spend an evening, I can tell you," said Isla as she waded with

Clova across the pool to where Pete and Bill were waiting, delighted to see her.

As they left the base of the mountain, Clova glanced back. The rest of Search and Rescue followed behind them in a procession of lights that rivalled the brightest stars above. Clova faced forward. They had a challenging journey over the moors back to the Drovers. Tatty stuck close by, not letting her out of his sight for a second.

CHAPTER 19

Clova woke with a start. She groaned as she sat up and switched on the lamp.

Tatty was nowhere to be seen.

The events of last night came back to her. Clova had been so tired after crossing the moors that she had gone straight to bed as soon as she had arrived home. She'd fallen asleep before her head had hit the pillow.

She checked her clock. It was eleven thirty in the morning. She'd slept in. Clova got herself dressed, wincing at the stiffness in her arms and legs. Her bruises were the same colour as the rock she'd fallen on. She pulled on some socks and made her way down to the kitchen.

Clova took a long drink of water and wiped her mouth. As she gazed out at Ben Attrin, she saw the reflection in the glass of her dad standing behind her.

She turned to face him.

Her dad drew her in for a hug. Clova could feel he was just skin and bones under his woollen jumper. They stood like this for a while, until he finally let her go.

"Isla said you managed to find shelter."

"Mum showed me where to go. She drummed into me that it was always better to wait it out than to push on if the conditions weren't right." Clova sat at the table where her dad joined her.

Her dad smiled a sad smile. "Your mum is still keeping you safe, even though she's not here any more." His voice cracked. "I can't seem to do that. I thought I'd lost you too." He turned his gaze upwards in an attempt to stop the tears spilling from his eyes. "Why did you run off like that? You scared the living daylights out of us."

Clova hated that he was so upset. "I didn't mean what I said to you yesterday."

"I know. I know."

"It feels like I'm a prisoner sometimes. You don't want me going outside because it's unsafe."

"Can you blame me after yesterday? Why did you go on to the mountain of all places?"

"I wasn't really thinking."

He didn't shout at her. He didn't even give her that killer look of his when he'd reached the end of his tether. Finally, he was listening to her.

Clova continued on. "When I'm outdoors, things come back to me about her. I can hear Mum's laughter. Remember conversations we had. She's not in a graveyard or somewhere up in the clouds – she's right beside me."

Dad's head bowed. He looked as though he needed rescuing right now. He was so lost in his thoughts.

"I am sorry I didn't tell you about Tatty. Grandpa was one who badgered me to talk to you about it, but I didn't listen. And now he's had to move out because of me."

"He's the grown-up. He should have known better. After everything we've been through, why did you lie to me?"

Clova couldn't look her dad in the eye. "Tatty took

my mind off Mum for a little while each day. He gave me hope there could be some happiness in my life again. If I'd told you about Tatty, I knew you'd put a stop to me seeing him."

Her dad appeared so fragile. As though he could crumble to ash the same way a log does in a roaring fire. "The dog was here, late yesterday afternoon."

"Tatty came to the Drovers?"

"I didn't know it was him. Mrs Cairncross had phoned your grandpa and asked him to keep an eye out for Tatty as he'd escaped from the barn. I wasn't sure who the dog belonged to, so I shooed him away."

"He must have tracked me from here to the waterfall. If it hadn't been for Tatty, Search and Rescue wouldn't have found me so fast. His barking alerted Isla." Clova picked at a hangnail on her finger. It was now or never. "Can I keep Tatty, Dad? Please? You wouldn't even notice he's here. I'll take good care of him."

"I can see he means the world to you – but I have enough to deal with. You know how much it takes to run this place. I'm stretched to breaking point as it is. I cannot cope with anything else right now."

"I'll do all the walking, feeding and training."

"And when you're at school? Or when you want to hang out with Sally? I'd have to step in to help and that's just not something I'm capable of doing at the moment. I'm sorry, Clova. I know this isn't what you want to hear."

Clova had run out of fight. There was nothing else she could do or say to change his mind. The time had come to face the facts: she and Tatty could never be together.

Dad stood and walked over to the window. "It's the anniversary next week."

One year since Mum died, she thought. It felt as though she'd been gone a lifetime and mere seconds, all at once. The anniversary would be a day that would bring their loss into sharp focus. Clova wasn't sure her dad was ready for it – that either of them were ready for it. How could they be?

Clova's throat burned as she stared at her dad's back. Everything felt like a battle right now. Her dad fixed his eyes on Ben Attrin. He hadn't noticed that she had got to her feet. Just as she was about to leave, the door opened and Grandpa and Isla walked in.

"Hello, odd socks! Mind if we join you?" asked Grandpa.

Clova ran to hug him. "I thought you'd gone!" When she stepped back she noticed she was wearing one sock with stars on it and one with blue stripes.

"I was needed here last night, but I'll leave today. The pair of you could do with some space. I'm truly sorry for everything that has happened," said Grandpa. He pulled out a chair for Isla to sit on.

There was a long silence before Clova's dad spoke. "Everything got a bit heated yesterday, which I apologize for. I … we both need you here, Archie, if I can persuade you to stay?" said her dad, finally shifting his gaze away from the mountain.

"Please say, 'yes', Grandpa," pleaded Clova as she sat back down at the table. She felt so bad she'd caused so much trouble.

"Och, I'd be lost without the pair of you. Besides, I am rubbish at packing. Think there's one shoe, a towel and a cushion in my suitcase," Grandpa grinned, winking at Clova. "And, for the record, no more secrets."

"That's settled then," said her dad, without hesitation.

"Actually there's something we want to run past

you both." Grandpa gave Isla a sideways glance. She smiled at him in a reassuring way. He continued on. "It's not every dog who shows the potential for tracking people that Tatty does. He's gifted. There's no doubt about it. Isla and I feel that it would be wrong to pass up a chance like this."

Clova sat bolt upright.

Her dad shook his head. "I've just explained to Clova that I can't take on the responsibility. Not at the moment."

Isla slapped her hand down on the table out of excitement. "That's the beauty of it. You won't have to. I will."

Clova couldn't believe her ears.

"Rannoch is due to retire soon and I've already raised the issue of training up a new dog with Search and Rescue. I think we've found the perfect candidate. Tatty's young, bright, energetic, a great tracker and from what I've seen so far – he loves the work. What Clova has done with him in such a short space of time is remarkable. I think with lots more training, he could be a good fit for the team." She leant forward to speak out of the side of her mouth. "Don't tell

Rannoch but I think he could have some serious competition."

"At the very least, we would like the chance to see if Clova's right about him," said Grandpa.

Isla nodded enthusiastically.

"And if not?" asked Clova.

Isla shrugged. "Whatever happens, he'll have a home at my farm."

Her dad scratched his stubble as he mulled it over.

Clova's face fell. She didn't want Tatty to go to the rehoming centre, but if Isla trained him up, Tatty wouldn't be Clova's any more. He'd only want to be with Isla.

Her cheeks reddened at such thoughts. She knew Isla and Grandpa were trying to help her *and* Tatty. Yet she had a sinking feeling she was on the verge of losing Tatty all over again. That they would never belong together.

Her grandpa waited for Clova to say something.

"You can see Tatty whenever you want. And with your dad's permission, you could help me with his training," said Isla.

"As long as there was nothing risky involved,"

chipped in her dad.

"Goes without saying, Jim. It means Tatty would have a forever home, Clova. He could help around the farm and he'd have lots of doggy companions. The fire's on every night at the farmhouse and there's a space on the rug with his name on it – if you're OK with that?" said Isla.

Grandpa glanced at Clova and then her dad. "What do you say?"

"It's not my decision to make," said her dad.

"Is Tatty here?" Clova finally asked.

"He's out the back with Rannoch," said Isla.

She got to her feet and left the kitchen. She tore down the corridor to the back door and hopped around as she put on her boots. Clova flung the door open and ran to the field. Rannoch barked and limped over to her. His foot had been bandaged and he had a white plastic cone around his neck to stop him from nibbling his stitches. She knelt and stroked his back. Tatty bounded towards her with his tail in the air and tucked himself in on her other side. He put a paw on her leg. His eyes shone in a way they never had in the barn. He was happy.

Clova couldn't bear for him to be sent off to the

rehoming centre. The thought of never seeing him again filled her with dread. What was the point of Tatty waiting around in a kennel for someone to love him, when she already did? She never wanted to be parted from him again. And if that meant Isla taking him then it was something she'd have to learn to live with. She watched as Tatty trotted over to Rannoch and stuck his head inside the cone. Rannoch pawed Tatty, who jumped back, sneezed, and play-bowed.

She had to put her own feelings aside and think about what was best for him.

Grandpa, Isla and Dad were up at the window, watching. She stood and nodded at them. Isla clapped her hands and Grandpa looked delighted. Her dad continued to stare. It took Clova a moment to realize he wasn't looking at her. He was gazing at the mountain behind her.

CHAPTER 20

Clova spotted the vase on the kitchen table immediately. It was filled with long stems of willowy green leaves. In the centre of the arrangement were six large clusters of rowan berries. Some of them had dropped off and lay on the kitchen table. For a split-second, she wondered if her mum was there. This was something she would do to cheer the place up. That's when she remembered today was the anniversary of her mum's death.

The colour of the berries reminded Clova of her mum's jacket. Blood red against the white of the snow on the day her mum had promised that she'd be home.

Has it really been a year today? she thought.

The walls of the Drovers began to close in. The mountain cast a shadow over the hotel. She felt a pang for Tatty. For the past week, Isla had brought him to the hotel every afternoon. He'd leap from the Land Rover and race towards Clova to greet her as if he hadn't seen her in months. If Isla was doing some training, she'd ask if Clova wanted to join in. In one of the exercises, they'd hidden Grandpa's slipper in some long grass and given him the other one to scent. He'd found it almost immediately. They'd even covered Clova in a light layer of snow. After a false start, he'd located her and didn't think twice about digging down to find her. When Isla ran through the basic commands, Tatty would do what was asked of him and then tuck himself in at Clova's side, not Isla's. They then decided it would be best if she came along at the end of the session when Isla always gave Tatty and Clova time together.

Clova loved seeing Tatty. With him, she could access a world that was free from misery – until, at the end of each visit, she had to watch him leave with Isla. Her heart would sink like a stone being thrown into a loch. And she'd, once again, feel the vast empty space in her life that her mum had left behind.

Grandpa came into the kitchen in a hurry, looking for something. As he grabbed a pile of paper napkins, he spotted her staring at the vase. "They're bonnie. Add a bit of colour to the place."

"Did you do this?" she asked.

"Your dad was up early. He cut them from the trees at the front."

Clova grabbed a glass from the cupboard, filled it with water and gulped it down. As she stared at Ben Attrin, she lost her appetite.

"It was snowing hard last night, but the temperature has risen and it's on the thaw. I've told all the guests there's a warning out for avalanches and there's a weather front on its way later. Everyone has filled out their walking routes, so that's something. I just hope no one takes any risks. Not today."

Clova didn't want Search and Rescue on any call-outs either. Her mum's accident would be weighing heavily on their minds too.

Grandpa hovered beside her. "Are you OK? Would you like me to phone school? Tell them you're not coming in? I'm sure they'd understand."

If Clova stayed at the hotel, she'd only mope around – and she doubted her dad would allow her to roam outside. And she couldn't hang out with Tatty as he was with Isla. Perhaps her classes would help take her mind off everything. "It's OK, Grandpa. I'll go in."

"As you wish. I'm going to the graveyard later on. Do you want to come too?"

Clova hesitated.

"You don't have to," he said, gently.

"I don't think I will."

Marie hollered down the corridor for Grandpa.

"That's OK. You should go when you're ready, not when you think you ought to," he said.

Clova put on the red coat, a woollen hat and a scarf. Before she left she poked her head around the door of the bar. Dad was nowhere to be seen. She headed outside wishing she was going for a walk on the moors with Tatty. Clova wondered what the collie would be up to as she left a trail of footprints behind her in the snowy car park on her way to the bus stop.

*

School hadn't proved a welcome distraction. Clova couldn't concentrate in class and had found herself staring at Ben Attrin in the distance. At lunchtime, she couldn't even face going to the library. Instead she moped around the school grounds feeling miserable. Nothing could lift the gloom that had settled over her. The loss of her mum came back to her in waves as if it had just happened all over again. She missed her mum brushing her hair and telling her about all the local folklore. And how they would cook wonky pizza together every Friday night with their favourite tunes on. Her mum had a way of making her laugh even when she'd been grumpy. She longed for one of her mum's hugs, which were warm and comforting and always made everything better. Her mum had made her world a wonderful and exciting place to be – where Clova had felt capable of anything.

On the way home, Clova had jumped on a bus that got stuck behind a gritter. It seemed the faster she'd wanted the day to pass, the more it slowed down. She ached to see Tatty. Finally, she was dropped off on the main road. She hopped over a mound of grey snow and crossed the bridge. The light was beginning to fade.

This time last year Mum was still alive, she thought.

Her breath escaped from her in clouds. As she walked into the Drovers she noticed the fire in reception wasn't lit, which was unusual. Grandpa and Dad must have been busy.

Clova spotted her grandpa in the dining room, speaking into his walkie-talkie. She dropped her bag and stood in the doorway. Grandpa had spread out a map on the table. She waited until he'd signed off.

"What's going on, Grandpa?" she asked.

"Oh, Clova. There you are. A climber has had a fall. The helicopter has taken Pete and Bill up the mountain."

She pushed down the feeling of panic. "Where are they?"

"At the base of Church Buttress."

Clova pulled a face. Church Buttress was a large rock formation near the top of Ben Attrin that was notoriously hard to climb. Many mountaineers came from all over Britain and abroad to set new records for the fastest route up it – except the mountain often had other ideas.

"They're working as quickly as they can but the fall has been an awkward one and the climber is stuck on a ledge." Grandpa saw the worried look on her face. "He's got a fighting chance, Clova. His friend was able to raise the alarm quickly. The helicopter will mean they can get to the scene fast and the ambulance is on its way. Things could have been much worse."

Clova glanced at Ben Attrin through the window. There was a steeliness about it – the snow appearing more bluish in the dying light. The mountain wasn't giving away any clues as to what it had in store for those who dared to venture on to it.

"Where's Isla?"

"She'll be here any minute. Come on, let's get a cup of tea. You look as though you could do with one."

They left the dining room and said their hellos to a couple of the guests going up the stairs. Grandpa put his arm round Clova's shoulder and gave her a squeeze. "How was your day?"

"Should have stayed home."

"I think you'd have felt the same wherever you were."

As they entered the kitchen, Clova noticed the white vase on the table was empty. Some of the berries still sat on the table. She picked one of them up and rolled it between her thumb and finger. On top of everything else, the rescue was bound to have her dad's nerves on edge. "How's Dad taking all this?"

Her grandpa had placed the walkie-talkie on the table and busied himself making a pot of tea. "I'm sure he'll be fine."

She frowned, puzzled. "Is he in his room?" she asked.

Her grandpa switched off the kettle and poured the boiling water into two mugs. Steam rose up. "He's out."

"Where?"

"Didn't leave a note."

Her grandpa stirred the tea, squeezing the teabags with the spoon.

She glanced at the empty vase. "Do you think he took the leaves and berries?"

"He must have. He's not been in the bar today. Marie stayed to cover for him." Grandpa brought the mugs over to the table.

"Maybe he went to visit Mum?"

Her grandpa shook his head. "I was in Glenstrome this afternoon. Nothing has been placed on your mum's grave – except for the flowers I put there."

She thought about this for a minute or two. "Have you tried his phone?"

"Aye, I did. The ringing led me straight to his coat in the cloakroom where he'd left it."

Clova cast her mind back to yesterday. Her dad had been so fragile when she'd told him she felt close to her mum out on the moors. He'd practically faded away in front of her eyes. She regretted telling him she'd wished it had been him in the accident, not her mum. "Grandpa? I'm worried I've hurt Dad's feelings."

"We all say things we don't mean in the heat of the moment." Grandpa sighed. "He probably just needs a bit of space today. I don't think there's anything to worry about. He'll show up when he's good and ready."

Clova wasn't so sure. Her dad hadn't seemed himself yesterday. But then again, he hadn't been the same since the accident. She sipped her tea.

A bell tinged in reception. Grandpa put his mug down. "I promised the Christies in Room 7 I'd give them a map of the area." He placed the walkie-talkie in his pocket and left the kitchen. A few moments later she heard him making the guests laugh. How her grandpa could act like everything was OK was beyond her.

Clova stuck her head around the bar door. Marie had lit the fire and there were a few guests taking advantage of the speciality whiskies. She waved at her before she hurried past the guests in reception and raced up to her dad's room. She knocked on the door, which swung open by itself. She clicked on the light. Clova noticed the curtains were open for the first time in a year. Everything had been left neat and tidy. She walked over to the wardrobe. Her eye was drawn to her mum's clothes. Clova picked up an Aran sweater and held it to her face. She could smell Mum's perfume on it. Her eyes filled up as her mind tricked her for a second that her mum was still here. She put the jumper back and crouched down. At the rear of the cupboard was where her dad kept his rucksack from the days he used to go walking. She searched around everywhere but it had gone. As she closed the bedroom door, a black ball of fur galloped along the landing towards her. Tatty sat by her feet, his tail wagging furiously. Clova knelt and Tatty lowered his head in readiness for a neck rub.

"Am I glad to see you," she said. The collie put his paw on her leg. His amber eyes calmed her. "Come on."

Clova stood and ran down the stairs with Tatty hot on her heels. She turned the corner, heading for the cloakroom. There she could see her dad's boots had gone and he'd taken his orange puffer jacket. Mum used to say it was so bright he'd be visible from outer space.

Concerned about the whereabouts of her dad, she went to find Isla and Grandpa. She didn't have far to look. They were in the dining room poring over the map. Tatty ran into the room after her.

"Hi, Clova!" Isla gave her a warm smile.

"Any news?" Clova asked.

"They're preparing to evacuate the climbers, which is great," said Isla. "Looks like backup won't be needed after all."

Clova lingered by the doorway.

"Grandpa? Can I have a word?"

He straightened up.

"Dad's rucksack and climbing boots are gone. You said yourself that he'd left his phone in his coat – but his orange puffer jacket and hat aren't here. Also, the car is outside. I'm worried he's gone on to the mountain."

Her Grandpa was perplexed. "Clova, what would your dad be doing on Ben Attrin? He's hardly been able to look at it since the accident."

"He couldn't take his eyes off it yesterday. I know he's really scatty with orders – but he's never left the bar without cover before."

"I think we could forgive him for absent-mindedness today," said Grandpa.

Isla leant against a table. "Where do you suppose he might have gone?"

Clova shrugged. "Wherever he is, he's taken a bunch of rowan berries and leaves with him."

"Your mum's favourite's," said Grandpa, softly.

"You were pretty sure he hadn't been in the churchyard." Clova paused, not really wanting to say the words. "Could he be heading to where Mum had her accident? That's what people do, isn't it? They leave flowers at the scene."

Isla and Grandpa glanced at each other.

Her grandpa shook his head. "He knew there was an avalanche warning."

Isla hurried over to the map, traced a route and tapped a point on it with her finger. "Pete and Bill are very close to Raven Gully. We could get them to check it while the helicopter brings the climbers off the mountain and then send the helicopter back up for them."

Clova paled. Nobody ever mentioned Raven Gully much. It was where her mum had lost her life. If she hadn't been so busy fighting with her dad, she might have asked him how he was feeling. Or what he was doing today. Or if they could do something as a family to remember Mum. Instead, she'd just presumed he'd be working in the bar.

Grandpa picked up the walkie-talkie. "Excuse me for a moment." Tatty trotted after him and then ran back to Clova.

She went to the window. The wind had picked up. It rumbled over the chimneys, blowing the smell of soot into the room. Sleet tapped on the glass as it began to fall in whichever direction the wind shoved it.

Isla joined Clova. Tatty lay down with his head on his paws and smacked his lips together.

"Whenever it was windy, my dad used to say that if we left the house it would follow us."

Clova's smile was thin. She put her hand flat against the glass pane. It upset her to think of her dad out there on his own.

"If he is on the mountain, he used to be an amazing climber. He knows what he's doing," said Isla.

Grandpa hurried into the room with the walkie-talkie in his hand. "There was a sighting of a lone climber at Four Rock Pass when it was still light."

"That's just below Raven Gully," said Isla.

"Pete said the person had an orange jacket."

Clova let out a gasp. Tatty nudged her and she stroked him.

"The helicopter is on its way down with the climbers. Pete and Bill have gone to the top of Raven Gully to see if he's there."

Clova glared at the mountain, willing it not to hurt a soul. Tatty whined, wondering what she was staring at. He jumped up to look out the window for himself.

Everything in the room flashed blue. The ambulance for the climber had pulled up outside.

Before her grandpa and Isla could brief the medics, his walkie-talkie crackled back to life and the helicopter pilot spoke. "Avalanche strike at Raven Gully. Repeat. Avalanche strike at Raven Gully. Two men down.

CHAPTER 21

Clova watched as the medics battled against the elements, taking the stretcher to the field. In the distance she could hear the faint drone of the helicopter approaching.

Isla flew into the dining room with her rucksack. She put on her Glenstrome Search and Rescue hi-vis jacket and head torch. "There's no response from Pete or Bill on their walkie-talkies. Any of the other teams nearby?"

"The Glenstrome Police won't be here for another twenty minutes – and the ETA for Ben Lovarnoch Mountain Rescue is forty-five minutes."

"I've spoken with the helicopter pilot. She reckons

we only have a short window before the weather makes flight impossible. We don't have the luxury of time on this one. I need to go."

"It's too risky on your own," warned Grandpa.

"Who says?" said Isla putting her waterproofs on.

"You don't have Rannoch. You'll only manage to sweep a small section of Raven Gully at best."

"A dog can search the same area as thirty people," interrupted Clova.

Isla and Grandpa stopped talking.

Clova's dad had been worried about her the whole time – and now it was him who was out on the mountain needing her help. She wasn't going to stand and watch – the same thing she had done with her mum. This time she was going to do something about it.

"I'll go with Isla and take Tatty. You admitted you had misjudged him and me. He can find them, Grandpa. I know he can."

Her grandpa shook his head. "Searching for people on Ben Attrin in these weather conditions is not the same as finding people on the moors or in the woods, Clova. If Tatty goes then it should be Isla who takes him. She has years of dog handling experience."

Clova put on her red coat. "Tatty hasn't bonded with Isla yet. He's bonded with me."

Isla glanced out the window. The two downward beams of light from the helicopter were now visible. "She's not wrong. Tatty's more likely to take instructions from Clova."

"Your father would never forgive me if something happened," said Grandpa.

"He won't be able to forgive you if he's dead."

"*Clova!*"

"I lost my mum out there. I'm not losing my dad. Let me go with Isla."

Her grandpa didn't know what to say to that. He raised his eyebrows at Isla, looking for backup.

"Told you she's a chip off her mother's block," said Isla. "If Clova wants to assist that's fine with me – but we can't hang around to discuss the finer details."

Clova stared at her grandpa. "Nobody wants to find my dad more than I do."

Grandpa saw the same blue eyes that his daughter had looking back at him. He recognized their strength and determination. And there was a glimmer of something he hadn't seen in a while: hope. That was what her mum always had: an abundance of hope and a courage that burned inside her. Clova had grown up with the Search and Rescue team. She'd listened to each and every rescue in great detail. She knew the drill. He doubted any other girl her age had climbed Ben Attrin as many times, in all weathers.

"You said bringing people home to their loved ones was in my blood, Grandpa."

He shook his head. He couldn't quite believe the words that were about to come out of his mouth. "Do you have the correct equipment, Clova?"

"She does now. Layer up," said Isla handing her a Glenstrome Search and Rescue hi-vis to put over her coat, a walkie-talkie, compass and map. Clova fetched waterproof trousers, a fleece, her head torch and rucksack, which she filled with extra gloves, a hat and scarf. She raced to the cloakroom for her boots. She pinched her dad's wool scarf and wrapped it tightly around her.

Tatty sensed something exciting was going to happen. Clova clipped his lead on and put his rope toy in her pocket.

Grandpa led them out the back door. "I'll keep on

trying to contact Pete and Bill. Stick close to Isla, Clova. Do as she says. Do not wander off. Keep alert at all times and stay focused. Radio in if…"

His voice faded away.

Clova's eyes were on the yellow belly of the helicopter as it came in to land.

Whup, whup, whup, whup went her heart.

She remembered how her dad's hands had gripped her shoulders so she couldn't run forward. The door had opened and a stretcher had been brought out. The blanket covering Mum's body had been pulled over her head.

Clova felt sick. Her knees buckled. Tatty barked at the helicopter, backing away from it. All of them were blinded by its lights. Snow was kicked up into their faces.

Clova froze.

Could she really do this?

Grandpa rested his hand on her shoulder, concerned.

A memory came flooding back to her. Clova's dad had turned her around and held her tight so she wouldn't have to watch the stretcher go past.

Dad.

On the mountain.

Alone.

Needing help.

Her help.

Mum wouldn't have thought twice about it.

She wiped the melted snow from her face. Clova crouched to calm Tatty. He tucked his head under her arm so just his nose peeped out. "Come on, boy. We've helped people before. We can do it again, can't we?" The collie whined.

The paramedics unloaded the casualty and rushed past. Grandpa led the uninjured climber towards the hotel.

"You ready for this?" shouted Isla over the noise of the helicopter.

Clova nodded. She just had to hope Tatty was too.

"Duck down. Once you're inside put the headset on."

Clova bent as low as she could to avoid the whirring blades and headed towards the helicopter. Tatty dug his heels in, refusing to budge. The noise must be terrifying for him. She fished a treat out of her pocket and gave the lead a small tug. Tatty stepped forward and she rewarded him. Clova lifted Tatty into the helicopter where he sat next to her, trembling. His ears raised and then flattened. His eyes were wide and he panted. She comforted him and put her headset on. Isla leapt in, carrying an avalanche probe and shovel. She closed the door behind them.

"First time in the helicopter for him!" Isla said.

"And me," replied Clova, whose headset came to life.

"Evening, ladies. Buckle up. It's going to be a bumpy one," said the pilot.

"Lynne Barton meet Clova MacFarlane. Clova MacFarlane meet Lynne Barton," said Isla.

"You wouldn't be named after the great Glen Clova, would you?" asked Lynne.

"That's right," said Clova.

"Fabulous place," said Lynne. "Unlike Ben Attrin tonight. We've got a northerly blowing in and visibility is bad. Since time is of the essence, ladies, and the engine has warmed back up, let's do this."

The helicopter rose from the ground. Clova

gripped on to her seat. The Drovers shrank and then disappeared behind a veil of sleet. It was hard to see anything as they gathered speed over the inky moors. The helicopter lurched off to the side, rose and then fell. There was a bang and a red light flashed on the dashboard. Lynne flipped a couple of switches and the light disappeared.

Isla saw Clova's face falter. She nudged her. "Rannoch is going to have a hairy canary when he realizes Tatty went on a rescue without him. He'll be in a right old huff for days."

Clova smiled. She brought her shoulders down from her ears. Tatty found his flying feet and stretched to sniff at some of the equipment.

"Once we reach the gully, we'll search the area with Tatty. Pete and Bill are wearing electronic trackers, but the signal might be weak if they're under lots of snow. We'll concentrate the search for your dad lower down the gully."

Clova's throat tightened. "Was that where Mum was found?"

Isla pursed her lips and nodded. "Clova, your dad might not have had the time to reach the gully.

He could have escaped the avalanche entirely and be sheltering until the storm passes."

Clova busied herself looking around the helicopter. She could see a first aid kit, a stretcher, splints, collars and a defibrillator.

"Clova, I need you to pay attention. There are two types of avalanche snow: powdery and solid. Powdery is good because it traps air, which means it's possible to make air pockets to breathe in. The solid type is more like wet cement and means less chance of survival. Should we get caught in one…"

Clova interrupted her, "Mum drilled it into me since I was six."

"Your mum was always very practical, Clova. Now you need to listen to me. Follow my orders at all times. Don't wander off. If the pilot says we have to leave, it means just that, Clova. Understand?" Isla wasn't doing her usual joking around this time. Clova had never seen her so serious.

"Got it." Clova pressed her nose against the window. She couldn't believe her eyes. They were climbing up a sheer rock face until a strong gust of wind pushed the helicopter downwards. Clova glanced at Lynne, who held the helicopter as steady as she could. The engine strained and the helicopter juddered before they shot back up again. Tatty yelped in fright. Clova called him over and talked to him in soothing words.

What if the mountain scared him more than the helicopter?

What if he ran away?

Mrs Cairncross's words came back to Clova: "*Malachy Bain remarked that the collie was a runner who attempted to escape so much he said the collie should have been called 'Houdini'.*"

Clova wiped sweat from her forehead. She wouldn't be able to chase after Tatty on a mountain in the dark. It would be too risky.

Every nerve ending in her body sparked.

What if she put Isla in danger? She was a schoolgirl whose mum had been killed on Ben Attrin. Did she really think she could help her dad? Or Pete and Bill? This wasn't a game she could play with Tatty. Lives were at stake, including her dad's. Clova's thoughts grew darker.

"Hey, Clova. Get out of your head. You've got this. You wouldn't be here otherwise," said Isla.

Her walkie-talkie sprung to life. Clova recognized Grandpa's voice immediately. "Casualty taken to hospital with leg and rib fractures. Keep me up to speed. Isla, don't let my granddaughter out of your sight."

"You got some soup on the go for our return?" asked Isla.

"Affirmative." The walkie-talkie clicked as Grandpa signed off the airwaves.

"Ladies. The wind's not playing fair. The snow's too deep. I can't land her so I'm going to balance on the rock. Should be enough time for you to exit. There's an overhang of snow at the top of the gully. Watch yourselves."

"Thanks, Lynne. Get ready, Clova and Tatty."

Lynne swung the helicopter in until the blades were centimetres away from the rock. They dropped down at an angle and Clova felt a bump as the runner of the helicopter connected with a giant slab of stone.

"*Go! Go! Go!*" said Lynne.

Isla opened the door. Clova took her headset off and shuffled forward. She felt a hand at her back shoving her.

"Duck, Clova. Duck."

Clova made herself smaller and jumped with Tatty. Landing on the rock, she slipped and crashed down. Tatty followed her, barking in her ear. Clova scrambled off the rock as fast as she could. She waded through some deep snow to put distance between her and the helicopter. Snow kicked up, blinding her. Everything was dark. She could have landed on Mars for all she knew. Isla threw out the avalanche probe and shovel and jumped. She held her balance on the rock and ran for cover. A split second later the helicopter rose up and flew out of sight.

"Has she gone?" yelled Clova in a panic.

"She's moved. She's worried about triggering the overhang. Come on! We need to hurry."

They headed for Raven Gully as fast as they could. Tatty was skittish. Clova remembered what her grandpa had told her at Stoneburn Farm. She relaxed her grip and tried to hide her fear from the collie. She patted Tatty's side until he focused his attention on her. She rewarded him with a treat, but he was too overwhelmed to take it. With her head torch on, all Clova could see in front of her was the sleet falling.

She pushed down her trepidation and thought about her dad, Pete and Bill.

Isla, Clova and Tatty entered Raven Gully. On either side, Clova could just make out the towering walls of rock, which afforded them a little shelter from the wind and sleet.

She stood, feeling like a fish out of water. Clova forgot what to do. Her mind went blank. She'd never heard the wind like this before. There were noises coming from the mountain she didn't think possible. Tatty's ears flattened and his tail was tucked between his legs. She could see the whites of his eyes.

Isla appeared at her side. "Get Tatty ready to search," she shouted.

This was not the time to lose it. Clova tapped Tatty, let out his lead and gave him the command. Tatty galloped ahead, barking. His head moved from left to right as if he was trying to work out where he was. The snow stuck to his coat turning it from black to white.

Clova commanded him again. He strained on the lead.

"Come on Tatty! You can do this. Go, seek!" Clova willed him on.

Tatty's head went down. He began to scent the snow. He stopped and whined, holding one of his paws in the air. He ran towards her and got under her feet.

Clova had not only overestimated what she was capable of – she'd done it with Tatty as well. She hated that Grandpa had been right. Again. Being on the mountain in these conditions was completely different to being in the woods or moors during the day. They hadn't prepared for this.

What had she been thinking?

Except Clova couldn't go back. She gritted her teeth and soldiered on through the snow. They weren't here to be scared. They were here to save lives.

They worked their way through the gully until they were halfway down. Tatty swung out from side to side, his nose barely connecting with the snow. Isla waved her arms to attract Clova's attention. "I've got a signal. Over here!" she cried out. The wind carried her voice away.

Clova and Tatty raced over. All of a sudden, Tatty began to sniff the snow. Clova praised him. He raced forward, heading to a spot near Isla. He barked and dug down. Clova spotted something green and bent to pick it up.

"It's Pete's gloves! He could be nearby," said Isla.

Clova held the gloves for Tatty to scent. "Seek, Tatty. Seek!" The collie began to sniff around again. This time leading them closer to the rock wall. He stopped and barked, his tail wagging. Clova praised him again. Now he was getting the hang of it.

Isla approached with the avalanche probe. She sank it repeatedly into the ground until it hit something. She handed the stick to Clova and began to dig down with speed. Clova, blinded by the sleet, wiped it from her eyes. She dropped to her knees to help Isla by digging with her hands. It wasn't long before they found a body. Isla cleared the snow from Pete's eyes, nose and mouth. His lips were blue and his eyes were closed. Clova sank back on her heels. Isla felt for a pulse. "We need to get him warmed up." She reached into her rucksack and cracked open some heat pads which she placed under his jacket. A pale pink colour returned to his lips and cheeks. His eyes fluttered opened. Isla grinned. "You owe me two bacon rolls with ketchup for this." Pete attempted a smile but began to cough. Isla dug the rest of him out with speed.

Clova's heart leapt for joy; he was OK. She fished out the rope toy for Tatty. He barked at her until she gave it to him. Tatty held on to it as Clova and Isla pulled Pete out of his snow prison. Isla gave him a spare pair of gloves as his hands had been exposed to the cold and wrapped him in a thermal blanket.

Clova found it hard to stand. The wind was blowing directly down the gully. The sleet stung her face. Her eyebrows had frozen and she couldn't feel her legs, fingers or toes. The wind gusted so hard, there were times it was hard to breathe. Clova turned to check the snowy overhang but was unable to see any more than a few metres in front of her. She grabbed the avalanche probe and tapped Isla on the shoulder. "We'll search for Bill."

"I'll make sure Pete's sheltered. I'll be right behind you."

Clova wiped ice crystals from Tatty's face. "Seek, Tatty! Go on! Seek!"

Tatty charged ahead, bounding through the deep snow. He stopped and whined, holding his back foot out from him. As Clova reached the collie, he curled up in a ball, whimpering. She'd never seen him like this before. She crouched to examine him. Small balls of ice had formed between the pads of his feet making it impossible for him to walk. Working fast, she warmed his feet with her hands so she could loosen the chunks and pick them out. Tatty's tail thumped off the snow. Clova fished around her rucksack. She found the spare scarf and ripped a section of it into ribbons to wind around his paws. When she'd finished, Tatty stood up. He tried to kick the pieces of scarf off.

She had to distract him. "Come on, Tatty! Seek!" Clova let the lead out so the collie could search from side to side and he soon forgot about his makeshift foot coverings.

Clova could feel her muscles tiring; she had to work hard to walk through the deep snow. Tatty wasn't picking up on any smells. They must be nearing the bottom of the gully by now. Bill had to be here, somewhere. Tatty changed direction, looped around her and scrambled back up the slope. Clova could see the faint glow of Isla's head torch behind them.

Tatty's nose dropped to the snow. The collie's ears shot up. He was on to something. Tatty halted, barked and began to dig. Clova dropped his lead and started to stick the avalanche probe into snow. After what seemed like ages, it finally struck something. She tested it again just to make sure. Isla hurried over to them with the shovel and began to dig down. A hi-vis jacket came into view and then waterproof trousers. Together they scooped the snow away from Bill until they'd uncovered his face. His eyes didn't open. Clova held her breath. Isla checked for a pulse and nodded. She dug around his body until she uncovered his legs. By the angle of his left foot, Clova knew it was broken. Tatty whined, sensing something was wrong. She gave Tatty his rope toy and praised him. Clova sank down in the snow. The wind tugged at her jacket and rucksack. She tried desperately not to imagine what it had been like finding her mum. Her eyes burned.

"Pete can walk, but I'll need help taking Bill back up the gully," shouted Isla as she began to warm Bill up with heat packs.

Clova glanced down into the darkness beyond. Her dad could be down there needing her help.

"We'll come back for Jim." Isla fixed a splint to Bill's

leg before she radioed back to base with an update. Isla then hooked her arms under Bill's and hauled him up with a groan. Clova had to trust Tatty wouldn't run off because she couldn't take the lead if she was to pick up Bill's legs. Tatty bounded up ahead until he disappeared and then charged towards them barking. Clova had never been so relieved to see him.

By the time they'd struggled to the top of the gully the helicopter appeared, dazzling them with its lights. Lynne landed it, balancing the runner on the rock again. They'd only have a short space of time to get Bill and Pete on board. They laid Bill down on the ground. No longer sheltered by the gully, Clova was caught off guard by the ferocity of the wind and fell. Tatty came over to nudge her. Scrambling to her feet, Clova helped lift Bill on to the stretcher and then into the helicopter.

"We have to go, Clova." Isla yelled. "Bill needs urgent medical attention. The weather's worsening. Our window is closing."

"I'm not leaving without Dad," shouted Clova.

"Do you remember when I told you that if Lynne said it was time to go, it was time to go? It's time to go!"

"I'm not leaving without him." Clova took a step back. There was a crunch and squeal of metal against rock. The longer they spoke, the harder it was for the pilot to keep the helicopter steady.

Isla turned away from Clova and shouted into her walkie-talkie. She covered her ear with her hand and listened for a second or two before facing Clova again. She pulled her in closer to her.

"Lynne thinks she can manage one more trip up. I can't stay. Bill has tachycardia: his heart might stop any second. Pete's hands have frostbite. Do you wish to remain here to search for your dad?"

Clova's eyes welled up as she nodded. She would do anything to find him.

Anything.

Isla gave her the briefest of hugs before she leapt into the helicopter.

"Isla!" Clova yelled, afraid at her leaving. "See you later, alligator?"

Isla slammed the door shut. Clova ran for cover as the helicopter left the rock and dropped vertically down the mountainside out of sight.

Clova's walkie-talkie began to hiss. She pressed it

to her ear. "Back before you know it, crocodile," said Isla, before signing off.

Even with Tatty by her side, Clova felt utterly alone.

CHAPTER 22

The weather was deteriorating. The wind shoved Clova as if she was nothing more than a piece of litter on the ground. She tugged the lead to get Tatty's attention and led him back to Raven Gully. She decided not to look at the overhang of snow. Best to pretend it wasn't even there. Clova gave Tatty the "seek" command. Tatty sniffed the snow and sneezed. The outer layer of his coat was beginning to freeze. No scent grabbed his attention. She stood, wondering what they should do. An almighty gust of wind tore down the gully. Clova's scarf fell from around her neck on to the snow and slithered away from her like a woollen snake.

She cursed under her breath as her skin cooled in an instant. That was her dad's scarf. In a flash it came to her. If she gave Tatty the scarf to scent they might have a better chance of finding him. Clova chased after it. She threw herself down over it, so the wind couldn't snatch it away. She passed it to Tatty to sniff. Now she could be certain Tatty knew the scent he was to search for.

Clova got to her feet and wrapped the scarf back around her. Her head torch flickered. Apart from the small strip of sleet and snow highlighted in front of her, she was aware of the infinite darkness around them. As she put her foot out, she stepped on sheet ice. She landed hard and, together with Tatty, slid down Raven Gully. She flailed around wildly to cling on to something. Out of the black loomed some rock, which Clova bashed into. She clung on to it to stop herself and Tatty from sliding any further down. As she caught her breath, she pulled Tatty in to feel his warmth. At least he hadn't been hurt in the fall. Exhausted, Clova rested for a minute or two. She took out the walkie-talkie and stared at it. She longed to hear Grandpa's voice, but didn't want him to know she was scared out of her wits. Besides, he'd be furious she hadn't evacuated the mountain with Isla. She tucked it away in her pocket for safekeeping.

All of a sudden, there was a noise above the wind. Like a train approaching at high speed. Petrified, Tatty struggled out of her arms and ran off into the darkness.

It dawned on Clova what the noise was. The overhang at the top of the gully must have collapsed!

Clova tucked herself in as close as she could to the rock wall, which would be safer. As she screamed Tatty's name, the ground shook. A tidal wave of snow slammed into her. Clova's ears, eyes, mouth and nose filled with it as she was dragged forward for what seemed like an eternity. Clova kicked her arms and legs as much as she could to swim up to the surface. As she came to a halt, she could feel the weight of it on top of her. There was no room for her lungs to expand. Clova thrashed around as much as she could, not wanting the snow to set like cement. She scooped out a small hole in front of her face so she could breathe and then pushed her hand upwards through the snow. It was what her mum had taught her to do. Clova shouted for help. She yelled until her throat ached and her voice was hoarse. All around her was an eerie silence. Encased in snow, she began to shiver. She had no idea how far down she was. If she was buried deep, her chances of survival were slim. Her thoughts turned to her mum and how frightened she must have been.

All of a sudden, Clova heard a scraping noise. There it was again. Something scratched against her extended hand. Clova must be near the surface of the snow. She kicked and fought to free herself from its vice-like grip. As she finally broke through it, she gasped for air. Tatty wagged his tail. He woofed and play-bowed thinking this was the best game ever. When she got her breath back, she handed over the rope toy, which he shook before dropping it. He decided he'd rather help her clean the snow from her face and ears.

Clova struggled to her feet. The cold had crept in through her clothing and chilled her to the bone. She wasn't sure she had the energy to sweep the gully all over again for her dad. She looked around to try and get her bearings. Fear gnawed at her insides. Clova had once asked if her mum ever got afraid when she was saving lives. Her mum had replied that she was greater than her fears. That everyone was.

For a split second, Clova thought she could smell her mum's perfume. The picture she'd been looking at on her phone flashed into her mind. Mum, Dad and her were all smiles after their climb to Four Rock Pass. It was a favourite place of theirs. They visited it so often they had nicknamed it MacFarlane Pass.

Clova gasped.

Her dad wasn't going to Raven Gully! He was going to MacFarlane Pass! That's where all his happiest memories of her mum would be. That's where he'd lay the leaves from the rowan tree. Clova went for her walkie-talkie so she could tell Grandpa, but it wasn't there. She checked both pockets and her rucksack. It must have fallen out when she was hit by the avalanche. She glanced back up into the blackness of the gully. Looking for it now would be like trying to find a needle in a haystack.

She had to get to MacFarlane Pass to check if her dad was there.

Buoyed up, energy surged through Clova's body

as she began to make her way down the last of Raven Gully. The snow was so deep in places she became stuck a couple of times. Tatty bounded over to check she was OK. Clova felt her way along the last of the rock until it began to curve to the left.

She knew she'd have to be careful. MacFarlane Pass was to the left of Raven Gully, but there were vertical drops in front of her. Tatty stopped to sniff the air, his ears pushed back by the wind. He bounded off before Clova had a chance to grab his lead. This was the last thing she needed when it was so perilous. Where had he gone?

Taking her time, she inched her way around the rock face. The wind tried to pluck her off the mountainside. Clova gripped on for dear life, knowing there was a large drop beneath her. Her hands began to shake. Then her legs. And then her whole body. She couldn't feel her fingers in her gloves or her toes in her boots. Her mind began to play tricks. Was she even gripping on to the rock?

She felt sick and dizzy.

She wanted to turn back. To crawl to the top of Raven Gully and wait for the helicopter. She couldn't do this. She'd thought she could, but she didn't have it in her.

All of a sudden, she heard Tatty barking. It was faint. But it was him all right. Tatty had found someone. She was certain of it. Clova willed herself to keep on moving. She had to trust she could do this. She began to shuffle around the rock until she could go no further. The time had come to step off from the ledge. She couldn't see what was beneath her so she stretched her leg down, checking for solid ground.

Nothing.

Nothing.

Something.

Crying out with relief, she stepped on to snowy ground. Not sure where to go next, she yelled for Tatty. He barrelled out from the dark and jumped up on her. Tatty barked again and trotted off, his nose to the ground.

Clova grabbed the end of Tatty's lead before he could do a disappearing act. Tatty weaved his way down the snowy slope, his nose to the ground. As he steered them past a large boulder, he barked. Clova couldn't see what it was he was reacting to.

She dropped the lead. Tatty took off towards a mound of snow and disappeared around the side of it. As Clova followed him, carefully, checking there weren't any cliff edges, she saw the colour orange in her head torch. The wind pushed her to her knees and all she could see was white again. As she wiped her eyes she spotted her dad, who'd dug himself a shelter in the snow.

"Dad! Dad?" She squeezed in beside him. Tatty wagged his tail. Her dad stirred.

"It's OK, Dad. We're here now."

Her dad attempted to speak. Clova held her ear next to his mouth.

"Is that really you?"

"It's really me, Dad." She held his gloved hand tight.

"You shouldn't be here."

"Neither should you."

"You sound just like your mum. She told me to stay awake."

Clova helped her dad to sit up. He was freezing, but not shivering which was a bad sign. She replaced his hat and gloves with the ones in her rucksack. Clova took off the scarf she had on and wrapped it around him.

"She's not really gone, has she?"

"Do you sense her here too?" She watched as her dad's eyes filled up.

"This was our favourite spot on the mountain. She came back to me. I didn't want to leave."

Clova hugged him and he hugged her back, not letting go for ages. Tatty lay alongside him to warm him up. She wondered what she should do next. She suspected her dad was suffering from the beginnings of hypothermia. She had to get him off the mountain, fast.

Her dad cleared his throat. "Did the dog lead you to me?"

"He did."

"Have you radioed the Drovers to let them know where we are?"

Clova shook her head. "Do you think you could make it up Raven Gully, Dad? There will be a helicopter landing at the top soon."

"I'll try."

Clova stood and hauled her dad to his feet. She placed his arm around her neck. His legs buckled and he dropped to the ground. Clova fought back her tears.

She didn't have the strength to carry him around the rock ledge back to Raven Gully. Yet if she didn't try, her dad wouldn't make it through the night. Time was running out.

As she went to pull him up again, Tatty barked. She wondered what he'd seen. Over the ferocious wind, she heard a familiar noise. This time it didn't fill her with dread. Two lights shot up in front of them. The snow and sleet was blasted in every direction.

Tatty backed off. Clova put her foot on his lead before he could do a runner. All she could see was dazzling white, until someone gripped her arm.

"Told you I'd be back. You and Tatty found your dad!" shouted Isla.

"I think he has hypothermia."

"We'll start warming him up as soon as he's on board."

Four members of the Glenstrome Police team appeared and assisted her dad on to the helicopter. Clova and Tatty scrambled in after them. The team worked fast to get her dad out of his wet clothes and placed heat packs around his body. He was covered in a blanket and strapped in for the flight. Clova had never felt as tired as she did now. She stroked Tatty's ears. As soon as Isla closed the door, the pilot swung the helicopter away from the cliff and they dropped down it like a stone. Clova closed her eyes and gripped on to her seat. When the helicopter held steady, she put a headset on and waved at Isla to get her attention.

"How did you know where we were?" she asked.

Isla tapped her nose. "I have spidey mountain rescue senses."

Clova wasn't buying it.

Isla burst out laughing. "I popped a transmitter inside your jacket pocket just so I'd know where you were at all times. That way I didn't break the promise I'd made to your grandpa – who is right royally upset with you, by the way."

Clova glanced over at her dad. Even though he was out for the count on a stretcher, for the first time since her mum's accident, she got a sense everything was going to be OK. That, together, they could survive her mum's death.

CHAPTER 23

The sunlight streamed through the library window casting a triangle of light over the table. Clova sat enjoying the warmth. Something she'd never take for granted again after her night on Ben Attrin. Clova heard voices whispering and opened her eyes.

The girls at the table opposite gawped at her. This time it wasn't because her mum had been killed by an avalanche. It was because word had spread like wildfire that she'd saved lives on the mountain. One of the girls gave her a wave.

Someone sidled over to her table, blocking her view.

Clova looked up. Sally put a book down in front of her. It was called *Goodnight Stories for Rebel Girls.* Sally cleared her throat. "It's full of tales about extraordinary women. I reckon you should be in there. And your mum."

She smiled at Sally, who grinned back. All Clova's worry and angst about their friendship melted away like flakes of snow when they land on skin.

"Fancy going for a hot chocolate after school?" asked Sally.

"If you're paying."

Sally snorted. "I walked right into that one, didn't I?"

"You did."

Sally hesitated. "When I heard what happened..." Her words trailed off. "I'm just glad you're OK."

Clova watched Sally leave the library. She felt a different kind of warmth. It was inside of her this time. All around her heart.

*

The waitress brought the hot chocolates to their table and slid them in front of the girls. Her smile was so wide Clova could practically count all her teeth. "It's not often we have a hero in our midst. The drinks are on the house. Extra cream and sprinkles too. You're an awfully brave lass, so you are."

Clova didn't know where to look. She took a sip of her hot chocolate.

"You've got whipped cream on the end of your nose," said Sally, pointing.

She wiped it away with her sleeve.

They didn't say anything for a while. It was a comfortable silence as they savoured being back in each other's company again.

The girls both spoke over each other at the same time.

"You go first, Sal," said Clova.

"I'm really pleased we're speaking again." She took a deep breath. "Sorry for being such an idiot."

Clova raised a hand in protest, but Sally continued on. "After your mum died, I wanted to do everything I could to cheer you up. At first it worked and I could put a smile back on your face. But then, without warning, you began to avoid me. I couldn't figure out why you'd rather be on your own. I thought you didn't like me any more."

Clova put her elbows on the table. "It's really hard to put into words what losing Mum has been like. It feels as though I'm in a fast-flowing river, clinging on to a rock for dear life, while all the time I'm in danger of being swept away by my sadness. I couldn't be upbeat and happy all of the time. It felt wrong. I took myself off so you wouldn't have to feel responsible for cheering me up. I didn't open up about what was going on inside my head – and for that I'm really sorry. I retreated into my shell. Please believe me when I say I never disliked you. I was and still am trying to cope with Mum's loss."

"I understand now, Clova. I really do." Sally fidgeted with her hands. "When I came out to the Drovers it was awkward because I got the feeling I was the last person you wanted to see. I must have come across as being so rude and uncaring not mentioning her. I never even asked how you were."

"You know, it's OK for you to mention Mum. I like talking about her. And if it's ever an issue – I'll be the first to say."

Sally's eyes filled with worry. "I had a go at you for wanting to save lives on Ben Attrin. I wish I could turn back time. I can be there for you, but give you space too."

"You're here now. That's all that matters. Sally, let's make sure that we keep on talking. I promise I'll never shut you out again. Unless you wear that pink-and-green checked coat of yours. It's *horrible*."

Sally stared at Clova. It took her a moment before she realized Clova was kidding and she gave a hearty chuckle. "Nothing wrong with that coat. I'm going to wear it tomorrow just for you." Sally stirred the last of her hot chocolate. "How's your dad?"

"Driving the nurses mad. But he'll be out of hospital soon."

"I can't believe you never told me you had a dog."

"Eh, we weren't speaking? Remember?" Clova put down her mug. "Tatty doesn't belong to me. Plus I'm not allowed a dog, so Isla has taken him in. He'll be trained up to be the next Glenstrome Search and Rescue dog, which is exciting for Tatty and the team."

"Won't you be working with him?"

Clova shifted in her seat. "I tend to be a distraction when he's training with Isla. Tatty wants to please us both, and that gets confusing for him. I've taken a step back so he can learn from the best."

Sally made her voice all posh like a newsreader. "You were doing more than OK according to the *Glenstrome Times*."

Clova flushed. Her grandpa had framed the article about her rescue on Ben Attrin and hung it next to the reception desk. He wanted all the guests to know just how courageous his granddaughter was.

"I can't believe I actually asked if staying out of town was boring! It's all going on at the Drovers. It's the most happening place to be in Scotland."

"Is that the new slogan for the hotel?"

"It should be!"

Clova couldn't help smiling.

"Do you see much of Tatty?" asked Sally.

"Isla brings him round to the Drovers every day. He and Rannoch are like brothers from another mother. The pair of them get into terrible mischief. They both ran into the dining room the other morning. The guests would have lost their breakfasts if Grandpa hadn't rounded them up and shooed them out."

Sally sat back in her seat. "You're so brave. Just like your mum."

Clova thought back to that night. The dark that had

swallowed her whole. The howling wind. The terror at being trapped under the snow. "I was scared out of my mind, Sal. I nearly gave up so many times."

"What made you keep going?"

"I had to find Dad, but it was Tatty who spurred me on. Here was this collie, in a hostile environment he'd never been in before, yet he showed me he had the heart of a lion. He never gave up. I couldn't either."

Sally leant forward. "What was it like saving lives on the mountain?"

Clova grinned. "Like winning an Olympic medal. Only better."

*

Clova had one more thing to do before she went back to the Drovers.

The gate shook as she pushed it open. The noise of it sounded deafening in such a quiet place. A blackbird glided across the green and white grass. Most of the snow had melted, but it hung around in stubborn patches where the sun couldn't reach it. The blackbird sat on the fence and *pink-pinked* a warning that she was there.

The paths in the graveyard were flat, but Clova

found this walk harder than climbing Ben Attrin.

The gravestone she was searching for was the one that looked brand new. Some of them leant to the side and had been so worn down by the wind and the rain, you could no longer read the names on them. Lots of them were covered in ivy. She wouldn't mind if some grew on her mum's grave. Mum always said that in the end we all return to nature.

When she found it, she saw Grandpa's flowers had fallen on their side. She picked them up and propped them against the headstone.

"I miss you." Her eyes filled up. She pictured the last time she'd seen her mum alive. Leaving the Drovers. Her coat red against the snow.

"You promised me you'd come back. You promised." Some tears trickled down her face. "And now I know you did. Thank you for telling Dad to stay awake. You're the only one he'll listen to." She half laughed and wiped the tears away. "I'm going to try my hardest not to upset him any more, Mum." She paused and reached out to touch the headstone. "I wish you were here. I wish Tatty was mine. I wish Dad would trust me."

Clova glanced up. The sky was a wash of dark blues, purples and golds. Ben Attrin would be magnificent in this light. The snow would be pink and the rock on its pinnacle golden. It would look magical and fierce all at the same time.

Clova checked her watch. The bus was due soon, so she said her goodbyes. As she walked back towards the gate, she knew her mum was on the moors and the mountain – but for the first time she could also feel her mum in her heart. No matter where Clova was, her mum would always be close.

CHAPTER 24

A balloon popped somewhere downstairs and there was muffled laughter. Grandpa and Isla had planned a surprise party for her. Except Sally had let the cat out of the bag about it by mistake.

Clova brushed her hair. Ben Attrin appeared friendly today, as if it wasn't capable of stealing lives. Isla would keep going on to the mountain with Search and Rescue and so would Clova. It was a place of beauty. And a place where you faced your fears. If you were lucky, you even got to conquer them. That's why their guests kept on coming back. It wasn't to put their lives at risk. It was because they felt more alive here than anywhere else. Clova understood what it felt like to help others. She would climb Ben Attrin again and again and again if it meant she could rescue people. Just as her mum had.

When she'd visited her dad in the hospital, they'd agreed to go out walking, together like they used to. And that every summer from now on – if the forecast was good, they'd leave flowers at the waterfall and MacFarlane Pass in Mum's memory.

Clova missed Tatty when he wasn't with her. But after the night on Ben Attrin, she figured she was lucky to have a collie like him in her life at all. Grandpa said dogs with a natural ability for finding people came around once in a blue moon. And that some adult handlers would never experience a dog quite like Tatty. If Clova was going to trust anyone with the collie – it would be Isla. Even the other team members couldn't wait to have Tatty on board.

Grandpa called up the stairs for her.

She left her room and trotted down to reception. There was a fire crackling merrily in the hearth and the place smelled of furniture polish. All the cobwebs had been removed and the pictures straightened. There was even a vase of flowers on the reception desk.

Clova hurried down the hallway, stopping as she neared the door. She was apprehensive about what might be waiting for her behind it.

She opened the door and halted as everyone in the room called out "*SURR-PRISE!*" Rannoch got up and wagged his tail. Clova stooped to pat him. As if sensing her slight uncertainty at what was going on, he settled at her feet, keeping an eye on the crowd.

Mrs Cairncross was holding a three-tiered birthday cake lit with candles. "This is from the hens. We miss you and Tatty at the farm." The Alsatian jumped up, keen to inspect the cake. "You'd better blow out the candles before Rannoch does!" she shrieked, holding the cake away from him.

Clova blew them out and the crowd erupted. Sally waved at her. The Glenstrome Police team popped streamers. Even Miss Willow was here. But Clova couldn't see her dad.

He's just been released from hospital. Maybe the gathering is too much for him, she thought.

Grandpa put his arm around her. "There's a couple

of folks who would like to say a few words on behalf of Glenstrome Search and Rescue team."

Pete and Bill shuffled into the clearing. "It's thanks to the courage of Clova and Tatty that Bill and I are still able to enjoy Archie's lentil soup and legendary bacon rolls," said Pete. The crowd laughed and someone whistled.

"This is for you." Bill hobbled over to Clova with a present and handed it to her. She tore open the wrapping paper to find a hi-vis with her name on the front and Glenstrome Search and Rescue Team on the back.

"You've got what it takes to be an exceptional team member and we're all very much looking forward to the day you join us. Ben Attrin will be a safer place for us, your guests, the locals and all those who wish to climb the mountain." Bill's voice cracked. Pete patted his back.

Words failed her. Clova glanced nervously over at the bar. Her dad was standing behind it. He smiled and clapped along with the others. She couldn't believe it. He was finally OK with her wanting to join Search and Rescue – something she thought would never happen.

Clova fought back her tears. She couldn't cry now – Grandpa would never let her hear the end of it.

"Before we get this party started, we have some more presents for Clova. If you'd do the honours, Jim," said Grandpa.

Her dad came out from behind the bar. He'd shaved and was wearing a shirt and tie. "There's one person who can't be here to wish you a Happy Birthday and that's your mum."

This caught her by surprise. She swallowed hard.

"You're so like her, Clova. You're brave, kind and smart. You care about helping people and have a love of the great outdoors. You don't do as you're told – something your mum never did either." Her dad paused at the ripple of laughter. He stood tall and looked her in the eye. "I'm so proud of you. I only hope I can be as good a parent to you as your mum was."

The crowd parted as Clova ran to give her dad a hug. When she let go, he led her to a table where there was a gift and an envelope. She opened the present first. Inside was a framed photo of Clova and her mum and dad at MacFarlane Pass. The very same picture that helped Clova figure out where her dad was. As she studied it, she no longer felt sad. They'd always miss Mum, but there would be happy times ahead for Clova and her dad. She felt certain of it.

Next, she tore open the envelope and took out a letter.

"Go on! Read it!" said Grandpa.

"Don't keep us in suspense. What is it, Clova?" shouted out Mrs Cairncross.

Clova stared at her dad and Grandpa. She re-read the note again just to make sure. "I've permission to start Search and Rescue Dog Training next year and will be the youngest to do so in the UK." She dropped the letter, which fluttered to the floor. Her eyes welled up. "Thank you!" Clova hugged her Grandpa, hard.

"Oh, lass. Think you'll need to go easy on the porridge. It's like being in the grip of a strangler fig tree," he wheezed.

Clova let go of him and spotted Isla pushing her way through the crowd.

"One last thing, Clova," Isla called out. "We all know you're going to make an exceptional Search and Rescue team member – but what use is all the training unless you have a dog to work with?"

A black-and-white collie darted into the room, barking. It took Clova a second or two to recognize him. Tatty had been washed and brushed within an inch of his life. His coat was smooth and shiny. His tail soft and feathery. Someone had even clipped a bow tie on to his collar. Clova dropped to her knees. Tatty sneezed in her face and tucked himself in at her side, his eyes bright.

Isla handed over his lead to Clova. "Happy Birthday, Clova!"

She squinted up at Isla, not sure she fully understood what was happening.

"You were the one who saw his potential when nobody else did. He belongs with you – not me," said Isla.

Clova craned her head round at her dad, who laughed at the shocked expression on her face.

"If you and your dad ever need a hand looking after Tatty – you've always got your grandpa – and me – Mrs Cairncross or Pete and Bill. Even Miss Willow has offered up her services. We can all make this work."

This was the moment she had been waiting for since she first met Tatty. Clova buried her face in his fur. He smelled of shampoo, but underneath the perfume was the scent of earth, sweet straw and warm buttery popcorn. Tatty's tail wagged so fast it hit against everyone's legs as he turned in a circle wondering what all the fuss was about. He jumped up on to an armchair by the fire and settled, making himself right at home.

After Clova thanked them all, Mrs Cairncross insisted she eat a slice of birthday cake, which was delicious. "I couldn't be happier everything has worked out for you and Tatty," she said. "Will you come and visit?"

"Tatty wouldn't be here now without all your help. If it's OK with you, we'll pop by tomorrow." Mrs Cairncross beamed. Clova gave her a hug to show there were no hard feelings.

"May I steal the birthday girl for a moment?" asked Grandpa. He handed her a brown envelope. "Malachy Bain dropped by earlier. He wanted you to have this."

"Me?" Clova turned the envelope over in her hands. She couldn't imagine what the farmer would want to give her. She opened it and pulled out a certificate. Written at the top was *The Kennel Club*. She looked at her Grandpa.

"Those are the legal documents for Tatty. You are now, hereby, officially his owner."

Clova was stunned.

"He'll have read about what happened and recognized the photo of Tatty. Who knew there was a big old softy under that gruff exterior of his."

Everything she had hoped for had come true. Tatty and her really did belong to each other now. She folded up the certificate and put it into her pocket. "Can I go out, Grandpa?"

He picked a piece of streamer out of her hair. "It's your party, lass."

Clova kissed him on the cheek. She worked her way around the room chatting to everyone until she spied Sally. She grabbed her friend by the arm. "Come on, let's go."

The girls left the noise of the bar behind, Tatty hot on their heels. Clova fetched her coat and they skipped out the back door.

Clova and Sally's faces glowed as they raced each other across the field. Tatty flattened his ears, raised his tail and zoomed around them. His coat ruffled in the wind and, much to Clova's delight, began to stick up all over the place in unruly tufts.

"Look at him! He knows he's found his *furever* home," said Sally.

Clova had been thinking exactly the same. Even though he'd been in a room full of people, he'd hardly batted an eyelid. It was as if he understood he was finally where he belonged.

"Have you had a good birthday?" asked Sally, grinning from ear to ear.

"About the best." Clova couldn't remember the last time she'd felt so happy. "I'm now Tatty's legal owner. I've got the certificate to prove it!"

"That's wonderful, Clova! Did you check out Tatty's name?"

"How do you mean?"

"You'll find out his *real* name. The one he was registered under."

Clova reached into her pocket and brought out the piece of paper. Her eyes widened a touch for the briefest of moments.

"Go on then, what's he called?" asked Sally, dying to know the answer.

"You'll never believe it in a million years."

Clova began to jog across the field. She spread her arms out and whooped until she reached the burn. Tatty tore after her and sailed over the water in one leap. Sally caught up with them, out of breath.

"Clova!" she puffed. "What's his real name? Tell me!"

Behind Sally, Ben Attrin rose up from the birch forest, quietly waiting for the stars and planets to spin around its pinnacle in intricate patterns of silver.

Tatty stood at the top of the embankment with his eyes half closed, watching over the moors and mountain before him. His coat gleamed in the last of the sunshine. He held his head high as he sniffed the breeze, which would be full of tantalizing smells freshly gathered from the land.

"Come on. Put me out of my misery." Sally pushed her hair out of her face and put her hands on her hips.

"His real name is Hamish: Guardian of the Glen."

"It couldn't be more perfect," whispered Sally.

Clova was excited at all the possibilities that stretched out before her and Tatty. Ecstatic, she took off again. It didn't take long for Tatty to catch up. He leapt up to nudge the palm of her hand with his nose, which made her laugh.

"Wait for me!" called out Sally. "Hey, Clova! Maybe I can help you with his training?"

"I'd love that!" hollered Clova.

Sally jumped for joy as Clova and Tatty weaved their way back across the field.

The moors had begun to darken in readiness for the night. Ben Attrin blushed copper and rose gold as the sun vanished in a final blaze of glory. Sally watched as Clova and Tatty's shadows lengthened until they became giants.

ACKNOWLEDGEMENTS

This book came about after my agent planted the seed in my mind. Thank you, Polly, for being the brains behind this operation. And thank you to Lauren Fortune for backing, supporting and helping me to craft this tale. I know how dear Scotland is to her heart. I have a million people to thank at Scholastic including Sarah Dutton, Catherine Liney, Penelope Daukes, Hannah Love, Kiran Khanom, Ella Probert and Jamie Gregory to name but a few.

Thank you to David Dean for such a gorgeous cover illustration, which brings the setting and characters perfectly to life.

Massive thanks to all the trainers, handlers, dogs and volunteers who hide for the dogs to find them. I am indebted to Jarlath Folan for his patience, kindness and willingness to help. It was serendipitous being able to chat about everything from dog training to what it's like when the pressure is on to locate a missing person. I would like to take this opportunity to thank Jarlath for the work he and his two Labradors, Syd and Shadow, do for Search and Rescue Dog Association Ireland.

You can't write about Search and Rescue in Scotland without mentioning Hamish MacInnes, who was instrumental to modern mountain rescue. Hamish and the Glencoe Mountain Rescue team used the local hotel as their base, which inspired the setting of this story. It was Hamish's novel *Call-out* which gave me a fly-on-the-wall insight into the many perilous situations they faced. Their bravery, indomitable spirit and good humour greatly influenced my writing.

To train and equip a dog and handler costs £5000. You can keep this vital work going by donating to National Search and Rescue Dog Association at nsarda.org.uk. Scottish Mountain Rescue have 850 team volunteers, who will respond at a moment's notice 24 hours-a-day, 365 days-a-year. To help them save lives, you can make a donation at scottishmountainrescue.org.

I would like to tip my hat to Bongo Fury and the Red Rocket for all the walks and plotting. And many thanks to my pal, Lilly Rea, for her fashion expertize and dialogue tips.

Lastly, thank you to Mum, Dad, Robert, Vince, Molly, Rowan, Finn, Nick, Kim, Amber, Heidi, Jamie, Monica, Oncle, Lee and Erin for your love and support. You rascals mean the world to me.

After backpacking around the world, Juliette worked as a creative for some of the UK's best advertising agencies. She became a Scottish Book Trust New Writer awardee in 2014. Juliette has been writer-in-residence at two primary schools in Glasgow and mentors children's authors for Scottish Book Trust. She is at her happiest exploring the countryside with her rescue dog.

"If you only read one children's book
this summer ... make it this one"
The Guardian

A brave, bright girl embarks on a heart-racing adventure to find her missing father – with magic and danger quite literally in the air... Twister's beloved father has gone missing and as she's searching for him, she stumbles across a witch living in the woods. She is given a magical necklace that holds the souls of living things and can turn the wearer into a wolf, or a rushing river, or a rainstorm. But there's a dark foe on the hunt for this necklace, a baddie who wears a coat crawling with creatures and who might have something to do with her father's sudden disappearance...

Every night Ollo goes to sleep willing something wonderful to happen, like flying out of the window and soaring over town, or galloping through a field of flowers on a unicorn. But nothing ever does: she can't dream. All the other kids at school have dreams. And they're not just ordinary dreams; they're enhanced, fantastical ones with a guaranteed nightmare-free adventure every single night. That's because there's a special place in town called the Dream Store, which sells every fun dream imaginable to those who can afford it, in the form of DreamDrops. When Ollo finally tries a DreamDrop, will she have the adventure of her life, or will things take a nightmarish turn...?